The Saint of St. Giles

Saints & Sinners Book 4

NADINE MILLARD

For Sharina who builds me up and never stops.
Thank you.

Prologue

NICHOLAS FYFE, ONLY living son and heir of the mighty Duke of Barnbury, stood quaking outside his father's office.

He'd never before been particularly scared of his father. Though the old duke was formidable, to Nic he was just his father. Distant, cold, and disinterested.

At least, he had been until Nic had finished Eton.

As soon as he'd returned to their main seat in Tipperary, Ireland, the duke had taken Nic under his wing and begun to teach him about his vast and many responsibilities. The cross of the Barnbury duchy was a heavy one to bear, and the duke expected nothing short of complete commitment from his son.

His daughters, they all knew, weren't of much interest to Lord Barnbury.

They would make good matches, as all daughters of dukes did, bringing honour to the family name and coin to the coffers. Not that Barnbury needed anyone else's money. The duchy was one of the wealthier ones in the realm, and certainly the wealthiest in Ireland.

But his son.

His son would carry the name, the responsibility, the honour, and the pressure of the dukedom on his shoulders one day.

Nic had always known what was expected of him.

And it had never bothered him. It was all he'd ever known.

Nicholas had always been level-headed and sensible. Always responsible.

Until recently. Until Ciara.

And now, here he stood on the threshold of his father's study about to tell the duke he was throwing away the life he'd been groomed for. The title, the money, all of it.

Because Nic had fallen in love with a girl of whom his father would never approve.

And so, he had chosen to walk away from this life of privilege to live with a young Irish maid.

His family would never approve.

And her family would never agree to her spending her life with an English Peer.

So, they would be on their own. Just the two of them.

It was daunting, but Ciara was Nicholas's first love, and he couldn't imagine a life without her.

He'd first noticed Ciara when he'd returned from Eton the last summer before he left to attend Oxford.

Returning home for Christmastide and summers in the years since, they'd fallen deeper and deeper in love.

And now that he'd finished Oxford and was due to remain at home in Ireland and begin to take on more ducal responsibilities, it was time to confess to his father.

Nicholas knew the duke would turn him away. But he had enough money to get Ciara and himself to England and for them to live frugally until he could find a way to support them.

He was an educated man and wasn't afraid of hard work. He would find a way to support them both.

Besides, he was one of a group of four friends who he knew would stick by him through anything. Robert, James, Simon, and Nic had met at Eton. Each of them destined to be a powerful Peer. Each of them different as night and day, but closer because of it.

A tragedy some years ago, one in which Robert's sister had lost her life, had only solidified the close bonds of their group.

If he needed them, Nic knew his friends would be there.

The time had come, and Nicholas had stood outside this door long enough.

His father had summoned Nic to a meeting. He didn't know why. But it was irrelevant. It was providence that his father should wish to see him on the same evening that Nicholas wanted to confess.

By tomorrow, he and Ciara would be on their way to Dublin and then sailing for England and a new life together.

Taking one more steadying breath, Nic lifted his hand and knocked.

"Come in."

A barked order.

This was it.

Nic strode into the room and stopped dead as he took in the scene before him. His father was seated behind the mahogany desk that had been his father's before him.

This wasn't an unusual sight.

However, Mrs. Jenkins, the housekeeper, was a surprising addition to the room.

Nicholas frowned in confusion as he observed his father's black scowl and the housekeeper's red-rimmed eyes and sickly pallor.

What the hell was going on?

"Nicholas, my boy, glad you could join us."

His father's jovial greeting was at odds with the tense mood permeating the room.

At odds with the housekeeper's obvious distress.

A cold, snake-like fear slithered along Nic's veins.

"You wanted to talk to me, Father," he said, keeping his tone steady even as his heart thumped with apprehension.

"I did," the duke said evenly. "Why don't you sit?"

Nicholas took the leather chair indicated by his father and sat back to wait. He had learned at a young age how to deal with his father.

The duke often sat across from someone in total silence, banking on their discomfort to force them into speaking.

Nic wouldn't be the first to break this particular silence. If his father had something to say, then he could go right ahead and say it.

The two men faced each other across the expansive mahogany desk, one older and overbearing, one younger and desperately trying to keep his nervousness in check.

The only sounds were the occasional sniffle from the housekeeper that the duke seemed to have forgotten, the crackle and hiss of the fire in the hearth, and the ormolu clock on the mantel.

After eons, the duke finally sat forward, leaning on his desk and pressing his fingers together in a steeple.

"A maid, Nicholas?" he said softly, and Nic's heart stopped dead in his chest.

"What?" he asked through white lips.

"Don't misunderstand," his father continued. "I don't begrudge you a dalliance with the help. In fact, I consider it a rite of passage."

Nicholas clenched his fists as his temper flared.

"But for God's sake, did you really think I'd sit idly by while you threw your life away for a servant?"

Nicholas's mind was jumping from one panicked thought to the next. He shot to his feet, his heart racing, his mind whirring.

"How did you – why did –" He took a steadying breath, though it did him no good. "What exactly is going on here?"

His father, in contrast to Nic's outrage, was as calm as ever and remained seated, an amused smirk on his face.

"A loyal servant came to me with concerns about your behaviour with the little nobody."

"Don't call her that," Nic warned through gritted teeth.

His father remained unperturbed by the censure and warning in Nic's tone.

He continued as though Nic hadn't even spoken. "And Mrs. Jenkins here was able to fill in the gaps."

Nic's eyes flew to the housekeeper's. Mrs. Jenkins had always been kind to him, always good-natured and jolly.

Now, she looked devastated and terrified. Nic knew without question that his father had bullied any information he had out of the poor woman.

He swallowed a lump in his throat before turning his gaze once more to his father's.

"I'm sorry you found out like this," he said as evenly as he could manage.

After all, he had intended to confess this evening anyway, so his father knowing in advance only saved Nic a difficult conversation. Why then, did it feel like he'd walked into some sort of trap?

"But I love Ciara, and she loves me, and nothing you do can come between us. We're leaving tomorrow, and we will be married. If you cannot accept that, then this will be goodbye for us."

Nic expected his father to rant and rave, to call him foolish and selfish, and remind him of how privileged his life had been. Even point out to him just what he was giving up, as though Nic weren't aware of that.

When the duke's icy calm remained in place, Nicholas grew even more concerned.

His father had never allowed anyone to question, disagree with, or doubt his authority. So, to remain calm in the face of his son and heir defying him? That gave Nic a worse sense of foreboding than anything that had come before.

After an age, his father spoke.

"Sit down, Nicholas," he said icily.

Nic remained standing. No longer would he bow to his father's every wish.

"I'm leaving, Father," he repeated. "*We* are leaving."

He turned on his heel and marched toward the door.

"But she's already gone."

The softy spoken words slithered along Nic's veins, freezing his blood and halting his movements.

He turned slowly, and his heart skittered in fear at

the smug look upon his father's face.

"What are you talking about?" he asked quietly.

The duke climbed slowly to his feet, peering down his nose at his only son, his face a mixture of self-satisfaction and disgust, no doubt at his son's actions.

"The maid," he enunciated carefully, as though speaking to a dimwit. "I packed her off last night."

Nic's eyes flew to the housekeeper's, and he knew from the despair on the woman's face that his father spoke the truth.

Ciara hadn't met him at their usual haunt this morning, but Nic had thought nothing of it. She couldn't always get away from her duties.

His mind began spinning as a feeling of nausea threatened to choke him.

"What did you do?" he managed to rasp.

"I've already told you, Nicholas," his father said coldly. "I was informed by a concerned member of staff that you were growing – attached to the girl. So, I had her removed."

"Yet you only questioned Mrs. Jenkins about it today," Nic interrupted as his temper flared. "What if your informant had been mistaken?"

His father merely shrugged.

"She's a maid, Nicholas," he drawled. "Hardly irre-placeable."

"She's irreplaceable to *me*," he bellowed. Still, his father remained unmoved. "I'm going to find her."

He turned to leave again, but his father's derisive snort stopped him once more.

"Good luck trying to find her now," he scoffed.

Nicholas's heart was hammering; he was struggling to get his breathing under control.

He felt as though his world were crumbling down around him.

"She can't have gone far," he spat, spinning back around and storming toward the desk, but even he could hear the desperation in his voice.

"My men were under strict instructions, Nicholas," the duke said calmly, as though they were discussing the weather. "She was put on a boat to England this morning."

Nic felt his entire body go cold.

Ciara had nothing. No money, no education to speak of.

To find herself dragged from the only home she'd ever known and dumped on a boat to England?

Nic's stomach roiled as he thought about what could happen to her, alone for days travelling, and worse, what could happen to her, penniless in a land she didn't know.

He sprang at his father, reached over the desk, and grabbed the older man by the lapels of his jacket.

"How could you do this?" he growled whilst the housekeeper watched wide-eyed.

Lord Barnbury reached up and pulled his son's

hands from his jacket, shoving at Nic's chest.

"How could I *not* do it?" he countered, his temper finally flaring to life. "You were going to throw it all away. Become a laughingstock. Drag this family's name into disgrace. For a maid, who couldn't keep her legs closed."

Nic lunged for his father again, but the duke wisely stepped back out of his reach.

"You'll forget about her," the duke insisted now. "Once you've grown up a bit, you'll realise I did this for your own good. For the good of this family."

Nicholas wanted to pound his fists against his father's flesh, but what would be the point? The old blackguard wasn't worth it. The only thing that mattered now was finding Ciara.

Taking a steadying breath, he looked his sire in the eye.

"If I don't find her," he promised, deathly quiet now, his anger having hardened to stone. "I will never see or speak to you again."

He turned once more and swiftly moved to exit the room.

"There isn't a chance in Hell of you getting her back," his father called. "Her or the bastard she was carrying."

Chapter One

Ten Years Later

NICHOLAS FROWNED AT the missive in his hand.

Ordinarily, he would be thrilled to hear from his lifelong friend, the Duke of Montvale.

Especially since Rob was writing to say that he was on his way to Town for the Season.

Only a few years ago, Robert would have died rather than come anywhere near London during the Marriage Mart.

But as with so many things from this last couple of years, Robert had changed.

His marriage to Abigail Langton, James's cousin from America, had altered Rob in a way that none of them had thought possible. Abby was a blonde-haired, blue-eyed tearaway. But she'd brought Robert back to life, and for that she would have Nic's eternal gratitude.

Inevitably, as soon as Nic's thoughts turned to Abby, they hopped right to the reason he was frowning instead of smiling at the news that his friend was coming.

Alison Langton.

His heart sped, much to his annoyance, at the memory of Alison Langton.

Abigail's younger sister had arrived last year from the Americas to stay at Montvale Hall, the main seat of Rob's duchy.

Instead of going to Montvale however, they had travelled to Liverpool at the behest of Simon, the Earl of Dashford.

When Simon had requested the presence of them all at a house party, Nic had thought the earl's years of debauchery and drinking had finally addled his brain for good. Simon was the last person on earth who would voluntarily host members of the *ton* in his home.

Curiosity and loyalty had driven them all to attend, with James postponing his honeymoon after his marriage to Senna Baker, in order to attend.

As it had turned out, it wasn't debauchery that had driven Simon demented, but love. He had fallen hard for the beautiful bluestocking Amelia Linchfield. Nic couldn't help his grin as he remembered what a match the feisty Amelia had been for the Devil of Dashford.

Nic had been happy for his friend, all his friends. He was happy when Abby had brought sunshine back to the Monster of Montvale. He was happy when Senna had shaken up the unshakeable Angel of Avondale. And he was happy when Amelia had sent the Devil demented.

What he absolutely, categorically was *not* happy about, was the fact that he'd have to see Alison Langton again.

She unsettled Nic in a way that nobody ever had before.

Not even Ciara.

Nic's heart twisted with familiar regret.

He'd come to terms with his past a long time ago. It didn't define him. Didn't trap him in grief as Rob's had done.

But that didn't mean he didn't relive it every now and again, that he didn't sometimes think about what could have been, if only he'd been able to find her on time.

Nobody knew the secrets of Nic's past. Not even his closest friends.

After that fateful night at Barnbury, Nic had fled to London as fast as was possible.

Mrs. Jenkins had confirmed what his father had said was true. Ciara was with child. Nic's child.

So, he'd dashed after her. But he'd been too late.

By the time he'd arrived in Dublin, the ship carrying Ciara and their babe had already left.

For years he'd scoured the length and breadth of London. Had sent men searching every corner of England for Ciara. Ireland, too, in case she'd managed to somehow find her way home.

It had been futile, of course. She had disappeared

without a trace.

Back then, Nicholas had been driven to the brink of madness by anger, despair, and loss.

He couldn't, wouldn't accept that he'd never see Ciara again. That he wouldn't ever know his child.

He never returned home. Never saw his father again, just as he had vowed. He stayed in London and threw his money, his time, his heart, and soul into finding her.

And then –

Nic flinched away from the painful memory that tried to surface.

No.

He never allowed himself to think of it. And he wouldn't do so now. It had been so long ago, and dwelling on it was futile.

The only way he kept his equanimity was by re-membering Ciara fondly. Not reliving the way he'd found out she was gone forever, along with their child.

Nic had seen first-hand the devastation caused by letting the past control your life, the way Rob had.

So, he had refused to do the same thing.

He had become stoic, calm, steady always. Never having his feathers ruffled. Never having his temper-ment be anything other than even at all times.

He dedicated his life to helping the poor souls around St. Giles. The very dregs of society in the Rookery. Around Little Ireland in particular. A place so named because it housed – and he could only use the word loosely – the people from Ireland who had travelled here either by choice, naïvely thinking a good life awaited them on the shores of England, or because they had no other choice. Perhaps they hoped life would be better in London. A mistaken hope indeed.

Though Nic had spent years of his life in St. Giles, he could never quite get used to the way of life there.

Though he spent money that would bankrupt a man less wealthy than he, he could never make a dent in the poverty and despair that hovered over the heads of the poor souls living there.

But he tried. Continued to try. And would keep on trying. For his own conscience, for the memory of Ciara, and because nobody with a modicum of morality could do otherwise once he'd seen the lowest depths to which a man, woman, or child could sink.

And if at night he still suffered pangs of gut-wrenching guilt, guilt that made him wake covered in sweat and reaching for a crying child, then that was his cross to bear and bear it he would, in the still, silent night. Without witness. And without complaint.

By day, he maintained his equability with little effort.

Or he had.

Until Alison Langton.

Last year, she'd burst into his life like a beautiful, distracting headache.

Nic couldn't even say why she had affected him so deeply, so swiftly.

He hadn't lived like a monk, so it wasn't as though he were starved of female company.

And he'd been around more than one beautiful woman. So, although she was an extraordinarily pretty thing, there was no reason for his heart to have slammed nearly out of his chest the first time he'd set eyes on her. In the brief time he'd spent at Simon's estate, Nic had felt constantly unsettled by the presence of the diminutive blonde.

He'd watched with a growing irritation as the male attendees had salivated over her.

He'd watched with unwelcome envy as she'd flirted shamelessly with Simon.

The worst part was Nicholas knew that had Simon not already fallen head over heels in love with Miss Linchfield at that time, he'd have had no problem seducing Miss Langton. He hadn't been known as a smooth-tongued devil for nothing.

And the fury that had raged inside Nic at the very idea had baffled and annoyed him. Perhaps even scared him a little.

And then there was that night.

The night of a formal dinner for the attendees of Simon's house party, where he'd found her alone on the balcony, and she'd bloody well kissed him!

Even now, Nic's gut clenched with latent lust as he

remembered the brazen brat throwing her arms around him and pressing those lips of hers against his, tilting his whole world off its axis.

The desire that shot through Nic upon contact with her had shocked him to his core. It was beyond anything he'd ever felt before. Molten, unstoppable, incinerating.

Now, here he stood like a statue in his own study, dreading the arrival of the chit and every stormy emotion she'd bring with her.

With a muffled oath, Nic slammed the missive onto the oak table that dominated his study.

What the hell was wrong with him, that he was allowing the memory of his brief encounters with the girl to get to him so?

It had been almost a full year since he'd last seen her, after all.

No doubt, he'd convinced himself she was more alluring than she'd been. Conjured an image of blonde-haired, blue-eyed perfection that didn't really exist.

No doubt, he was misremembering the desire, the interest, the pull of *something* he'd felt in her company.

Bizarre, given that she was everything he didn't particularly like in a person; privileged, pampered, and pandered to.

With his life dedicated to helping the most unfortunate souls in London, Nic sometimes struggled with the privilege of the world to which he belonged.

But he remained in it. Remained a part of it. Because the people of St. Giles and slums all over Ireland and England didn't just need his charity, they needed a voice in Parliament. And he was determined to be that voice.

Usually, he knew better than to judge other members of the *haute monde*. A lot of them, especially the wives and daughters, were involved in charitable endeavours. He never blamed them for their lot in life, for the privilege they were born to.

It was unfair then to hold it against Alison Langton.

Yet being irritated by her, critical of her, gave him an odd sense of security. A reason to keep her at a distance.

Again, his reaction to her baffled him. And if he were being honest, he knew she was probably no worse than any other beautiful young woman of the *ton*.

None of the other beautiful young women had stirred something long-buried inside him, though. And that was the problem.

But she couldn't have been quite as beautiful as he remembered. Her smile couldn't have twisted his heart in such a way.

Nicholas's racing heart calmed as he pulled his control around him like a cloak, tamped down any and all emotions, and regained his equilibrium.

Of course, he wasn't going to be affected by one

young debutante in the sea of debutantes preparing to fish for husbands in the Marriage Mart.

The Season was close to being in full swing. And Abigail and Robert were determined to throw Alison into the throes of it, according to Rob's note.

Alison had apparently expressed the same desire to remain in England as her sister had some years ago.

So, she'd hardly be around a stuffy duke such as himself.

No, she'd be off getting every red-blooded male in the vicinity to fall in love with her. She'd be as vivacious, and flirtatious, and superficially charming as she had been last year, Nic was sure.

But it was no matter. Hadn't he just decided he wasn't going to be affected by her?

Let her come and bring London to its knees.

Nic had long since given up any interest he had in the *beau monde*. He attended events because it was expected of him.

He would attend Parliament because he owed it to people not to abuse his good fortune to have been born a Peer. To fight for the rights and causes of the poor and indigent.

But that was it as far as being a member of the *haute ton*.

He would never marry. Of that he was certain.

He would continue to do the only thing that gave him any semblance of peace and something akin to happiness anymore; support financially and otherwise the various charities he was involved in around the Rookery of St. Giles and more specifically, Little Ireland.

And when he did see Miss Langton and realised that his mind had made her more beautiful than she possibly could be, he would regain his famed equilibrium in earnest.

Feeling far calmer than he had when he'd first read Rob's letter, Nic straightened his cravat and swept out of his Mayfair townhouse to the waiting carriage.

He had a busy day ahead of him. And he wouldn't be distracted by memories of a few brief encounters with a spoilt, Society miss.

Chapter Two

"ALLY, DEAR, IF you press your face any closer to the window, your nose will go through it."

Alison Langton turned to grin at her sister before pressing her face once more to the window.

She couldn't help it.

Finally, *finally* she was in London for the famed Season.

Alison had come out in New York, of course, but even Abigail had admitted to her that nothing quite matched the excitement, the pomp and circumstance, the sheer exhilaration of a London Season.

Having spent almost a full year at Robert's beautiful but rather isolated seat in Northumberland, Alison was more than ready to be swept up in the excitement of Town.

Not that the year hadn't been exciting, of course.

The arrival of Robert and Abigail's daughter had caused so much joy for both her parents and her aunt, that it had been enough to distract Alison from thoughts of London.

But as Charlotte Georgina had grown older, and

21

the Season had grown closer, Ally's anticipation stirred once more.

She wouldn't know many people, but Abigail had assured her that entry to the right places and parties wouldn't be a problem.

She was the sister of a duchess, only a step down from royalty.

"People will be begging you to attend their events." Abigail had said, rolling her eyes.

Abigail found the entire thing ridiculous. Ironic given the fact that she, herself, had convinced their cousin James, the Marquess of Avondale, to take her to England so she could enjoy a Season.

As it had turned out, James had taken Abigail to stay at Montvale Hall first, and Abigail had fallen desperately in love with her duke.

By the time Abigail had actually travelled to London for her first Season, she'd been in love with and engaged to Robert.

"It lost some of its appeal," she had explained to Alison. *"When it meant I was away from Robert."*

Alison sighed wistfully as they rode through the busy streets of London.

They couldn't be far now from Robert's townhouse. The streets were becoming cleaner, less clogged with people and roving animals.

And the buildings seemed to be getting grander and whiter with every turn of the carriage wheels.

She would give anything to have a man love her the way Robert so clearly loved Abigail.

It would be easy to convince herself that such a love was a fluke, if she hadn't seen the way James looked at Senna, his wife of two years now.

Or if she hadn't witnessed how the Earl of Dashford had become so desperately besotted with his now-wife, Amelia.

There's had been a story Alison had actually witnessed, instead of just hearing about it.

And though Amelia had mistakenly thought there was an attraction between Alison and Lord Dashford, ultimately, they had found their way to each other, and Alison had found her first true friend in England, outside of her family.

She hoped Amelia and Simon would return from their sojourn in Rome soon. Amelia was an archaeology enthusiast, and Simon was an Amelia enthusiast, which meant that wherever Amelia wanted to go and study ancient artefacts, Simon made it happen.

But they kept in touch through letters, and Amelia had assured Alison they would be back for at least part of the Season.

Alison was a little worried that her forwardness and inescapable Americanism would land her in ill-favour with the *ton*.

She would feel much better having not only Abigail, but Senna and Amelia on her side as well.

Robert and James had no choice but to support her, since they were family. And Simon had been kind to her from their first meeting and would, Alison was sure, continue to extend the same kindness.

The only person whose kindness she already knew she couldn't rely on was the last member of Robert's circle of friends; the Duke of Barnbury.

As her mind flitted to the handsome duke, Alison's heart stuttered.

Handsome didn't really do him justice, truth be told.

He was the most beautiful, masculine man Alison had ever seen.

And Robert, James, and Simon weren't exactly displeasing to the eye either. But there was something about the dark-haired, navy-eyed duke that heated Alison's blood in a way she'd never experienced before or since.

The first time she'd met him last year, her breath had caught in her throat and for the entirety of Lord Dashford's house party, she had felt unbalanced by him.

Which was terribly romantic and exactly what she'd wished for when she'd been dreaming of England and all its charms.

The intense dislike she'd felt emanating from the quiet, solemn duke had been rather less enjoyable.

Alison remembered in embarrassingly great detail

the exact moment she'd met Lord Barnbury.

They'd all been invited to Lord Dashford's seat in Liverpool, ostensibly for a party to honour his cousin. They knew now, however, that the entire party had been thrown so Simon could spend time in Amelia's company.

She'd walked into the beautiful drawing room of Simon's manor house, looked around with curious eyes, and landed on the most breath-takingly handsome man she'd ever seen.

Well over six feet tall, he was a comparative giant to her own five-feet-four-inches.

His broad shoulders had been encased in a navy-blue superfine, and her throat had dried as she realised the jacket was the exact shade of his eyes. He had lashes a lady would kill for, thick and black, and his chestnut hair gleamed in the afternoon sun.

Alison had known she was gaping rather embarrassingly, but she couldn't help it. Her eyes drank in the chiselled jaw, the strong chin, the solid chest under his snowy white cravat.

She had blatantly and thoroughly studied every inch of him, right down to the shiny Hessian boots.

But when her eyes had travelled back up and clashed suddenly with his own, her breath had caught for a very different reason.

At first, his gaze had flashed with something so scorching that Alison felt as if the look seared her skin.

But in the next instant he'd looked hostile, almost as though her mere presence had angered him.

She'd been left feeling rattled and shaken by the look and later, when they'd been introduced, he'd been coldly polite and nothing more.

In fact, for the rest of Alison's time in Dashford, she'd felt nothing but antagonism from the solemn duke.

Whatever madness had overtaken her on the night of the dinner, the night she'd decided that she wanted her first kiss to be with the sombre duke, it had only served to make him dislike her further.

For a brief, wonderful, earth-shattering moment, he had kissed her back. She was quite sure of that.

Though he'd pushed her from him, gently but firmly, though he'd stared at her as though she'd run mad, though he'd spoken not a word before he had turned on his heel and fled, never speaking to her about it or anything really again, Alison knew he'd kissed her back.

She knew because for almost every night since, she had replayed that moment over repeatedly in her foolish mind.

She had been thrilled by the encounter, having spent the entire evening building up the courage to do it.

By her reckoning, she had come to England to have an epic love affair with a dashing English lord, and she was impatient to get started.

In retrospect, it probably would have been best to at least give the man a clue as to what she wanted before attacking him.

But when he'd come upon her on the balcony, in the moonlight, it had seemed like Fate.

When he'd run away afterwards, it had felt decidedly less like Fate and more like she were some sort of predator.

After, Alison knew that whatever slight flicker of liking he might have held for her had been well and truly snuffed out.

Though he'd never said anything outwardly rude, to be fair.

And from what everyone said, anything other than politeness and gentlemanliness from the handsome Peer was unheard of.

That meant whatever negativity he felt toward Alison was reserved *only* for Alison.

That had been tough to swallow, and Alison would like to say it had cured her of her infatuation with the man, but sadly it had only made him more enticing.

Though it made her seem unbearably conceited, the fact was that Alison wasn't used to not getting something she wanted.

Even with her parents, who had little time for any of their three daughters, Alison had been coddled more than Abigail and their younger sister, Beth.

In New York she'd been treated like royalty by matriarchs, fawned over and flattered by dandies.

She'd never really encountered someone who blatantly disliked her...

The carriage jolted suddenly, bringing Alison back from her wandering thoughts.

Abigail's six-month-old daughter stirred, and both ladies immediately snapped to attention.

But the baby settled once more in her mama's arms, and returned to her deep, steady sleep.

"Ah, here we are."

Alison turned to take in the white stucco front of Robert's townhouse.

It was huge and beautiful, as Alison had known it would be.

Robert was a duke, after all. And rich as Croesus.

"James's house is across the Park," Abby said as the carriage rolled to a halt. "And Simon's is a short walk from James's."

The door opened, and a footman hurried to place a stool at the opening.

"And Nic's," Abby continued. "Is just there."

She pointed to another, equally large, equally beautiful home only steps from where their carriage sat.

Lord Barnbury was, of course, a duke, as well. Though his duchy was in Ireland, Abigail had informed Alison that he never went home. Not even for the passing of his father.

"So, he lives here in London all year?" Alison asked, keeping her tone casual.

"I assume so. Nicholas is never particularly open about what he does. He's a very private person."

Ali didn't want to badger her sister. Nor did she want to give away her foolish infatuation, but she couldn't help asking questions.

"And is he always so – serious?"

Abigail grinned.

"Robert said that he used to be quite different. According to him, Nic was as carefree as James and even Simon in his day, though perhaps not as badly behaved as Simon," she laughed. "Until about ten years ago. He said that one day, Nic came back from Ireland and was an entirely different person. None of them ever knew why, and he never said. But he doesn't tell them anything about his life, not really. Robert said there's not much to tell. He has kept them all in line when needed. Always been the most level-headed and sensible one of them. Lives a quiet and uneventful life."

Alison was more than a little intrigued and lapped up the information about the mysterious duke.

But it wouldn't do to let her sister know how fascinated she was by even this snippet of information. Abby would tease her mercilessly.

"Lord, how boring," Ally said jokingly, hoping not to raise any suspicions.

In any case, he *did* sound boring. Chances were

she'd made him far more interesting in her head than he actually was.

"What an old fuddy-duddy. I hope the other gen-tlemen I meet are more interesting than Lord Barnbury."

"I'm sure they will be."

Alison gasped and whipped her head back to the open door at the sound of a masculine voice.

"Oh, no," she whispered as she took in the giant shoulders, the glinting navy eyes, the stern expression.

The Duke of Barnbury stood there, stiff as a statue and glaring into the carriage.

And he was not impressed.

Chapter Three

S HE WAS EVEN more beautiful than he remembered.

Although Nic had convinced himself that his mind had smoothed imperfections, had made her more impossibly lovely than she could be, it turned out his imagination just hadn't been up to the task of doing Miss Alison Langton justice.

She was, in actuality, far more beautiful than his limited mind had given her credit for.

Her hair, tucked though it was under a straw bonnet, gleamed like gold in the summer sun.

Nic felt an unwelcome tightening of desire as he watched those damned kissable lips form a surprised "oh."

Her cheeks grew pink, her astonishingly blue eyes widened, and though he would have assumed they'd be filled with shame or remorse at having been caught speaking so ill of a duke, they sparkled instead with a mischief that set his teeth on edge.

Perhaps he hadn't remembered her beauty accurately, but he had certainly been correct about her irritating impropriety and mischievous nature.

His eyes darted to Abigail, who looked worriedly between Nic and the termagant, before moving right back to Miss Langton.

Nic felt the deep scowl on his face but was power-less to rid himself of it.

Every single thing about this woman annoyed him, and for the first time in his life, he had no qualms in making that fact known.

But rather than drop her gaze demurely or seem in any way contrite, her chin tilted up and a blue flame of defiance flashed in her eyes.

"Nic, it's good to see you, man."

Nicholas turned at the sound of Robert's voice.

Though it had been a couple years now since Rob had met Abigail, the difference in his friend still took Nic by surprise.

Gone was the haunted look in Rob's grey eyes. Gone was the air of pain and despair that had always seemed to surround the duke, drowning him in its oppressiveness.

Now, Robert's face was creased in smiles more often than not.

And the dark circles under his eyes were, Nic was sure, a product of the arrival of little Lady Charlotte rather than Robert's past holding him in its clutches.

"Ah, the new father. I was just getting ready to greet Abigail and meet Lady Charlotte." Nic clasped Rob's outstretched hand, clapping him on the back and giving him a genuine smile.

He didn't mention the other occupant of the carriage.

The occupant with the kissable though extremely annoying mouth.

Robert stepped around Nic and held a hand out to assist the ladies.

Nic should have done so, of course.

But he'd been rendered a statue, first by the sound of Alison Langton's insulting remarks, and then by the sight of her sitting there bedecked in blue velvet.

She appeared to be the epitome of social grace and innocence. Nic was sure she was anything but.

Shaking himself from his distracting thoughts, Nic turned in time to see Robert take his daughter from Abigail's arms and turn to face him, his face stamped with paternal pride.

"Here she is," he said, his voice filled with an awe only parents seemed to be able to produce, and only when talking about their offspring.

The lance of hurt that shot through Nic upon sight of the babe took him by surprise.

It wasn't often that he experienced the pain of his loss anymore. If he allowed it to, it would consume him.

And so, he quite simply didn't allow it to.

But standing there, gazing down at the bundle of pink and white, he couldn't stop his mind from going

33

somewhere he desperately tried to protect it from.

Would his own child have been tiny like this one?

Would he have grown to a sweet little imp like James's ward, Poppy?

These were questions he never allowed himself to ask.

Yet here he was, wondering all the same.

"Lottie, meet Uncle Nic."

Nic quickly gathered himself in time to first bend and place a quick kiss on Abigail's cheek, steadfastly ignoring her sister, before holding out his arms for Rob to place the baby into them.

All around them there was bustle.

Servants dashed in and out of the white-stucco townhouse carrying trunks and following the orders of the overseeing butler.

Nic barely heard any of it.

He gazed into the perfect face of the sleeping baby, and something splintered in his heart.

He was truly happy for his friend. Felt truly privileged to be considered an uncle to Lottie, and Poppy, and any other children who may come along in their small circle.

But he would never experience fatherhood himself.

Never wanted to.

And that decision, a decision made in the dank, dark hallway of yet another Rookery hovel, had never been one that he'd regretted. More than that, it was a decision he never thought about.

Yet, just like the questions he'd asked himself moments ago, the thought he had whilst he held Lady Charlotte Forsythe wouldn't be silenced.

What sort of father would I have made to the child I never had a chance to meet?

Before his emotions could foolishly make themselves known, Nic took a steadying breath and smiled at the doting parents.

"She's perfect," he said simply. "She must get that from her mother."

Rob laughed, his arm snaking around his wife's waist.

"I have no doubt that she does," he answered easily. "Certainly, her beauty comes from the Harrington side of the family. Just don't tell James I said that, or we'll never hear the end of it."

Nic laughed.

"He won't hear it from me," he said. "When he arrives at Town, you can tell him yourself how much you admire that pretty face of his."

Charlotte stirred, and Abby stepped forward to take her from Nic.

"She will be wanting to feed soon," she said, either not knowing or not caring that ordinarily, duchesses did not speak of such things to gentlemen.

"I'll come with you."

Nic's eyes flew to Miss Langton, whom he'd been

purposefully ignoring.

"You've just come to London, Ally. You can hardly want to lock yourself away in the nursery with me. Better to get all of the latest gossip from Nicholas." She grinned.

Miss Langton's eyes flew to Nic's, and he tried not to notice the flecks of silver in their bright blue depths.

Nic bit his tongue to stop from rudely telling her he didn't want her company.

He knew he was scowling again.

And he knew if he didn't stop, Robert would notice.

And if Robert noticed, then he'd tell James.

The last thing Nic needed was both the chit's brother-in-law *and* cousin, having a problem with him.

Because they'd ask him questions he simply couldn't answer.

Nic didn't know why he disliked the tiny blonde as much as he did.

Didn't know why he reacted so viscerally to her mere presence.

Her words in the carriage had been scathing, but he wasn't a missish debutante overset because someone didn't like him.

Though, he had to concede, it was rare for anyone to *dis*like him.

He might not garner the adoration James did, but he certainly had never upset or offended anyone.

But now, he was tempted to.

In any event, Miss Langton saved him from either being rude or having to endure her company.

"I think the reception in the nursery will be warmer than the one I'm getting here," she quipped outrageously.

She then turned her gaze up to his once more.

"I am sorry that you heard what I said earlier, your grace. About your being a boring fuddy-duddy."

Nic could have wrung her slender neck as he heard Rob's snort of amusement.

"That's quite all right, Miss Langton," he forced through gritted teeth. "I'm sure we all say things we don't mean at times."

His tone was gratingly condescending, even to his own ears.

He watched in trepidation as a spark of mischief flashed in her expressive eyes.

"Oh, I meant it," she drawled. "I'm just sorry I got caught."

He could only stare as she turned and dashed up the steps to the townhouse, her blue velvet skirts trailing behind her.

Chapter Four

"D O YOU WANT to tell me what that was all about?"

Nic sighed as he took the tumbler of brandy from Rob's hand then sat on a chair in the study.

When Robert's only reaction to Miss Langton's behaviour outside had been to offer a drink, Nic had thought the matter would be dropped.

Clearly that was wishful thinking.

Another black mark against the defiant debutante.

"What do you mean?" he hedged.

Rob merely raised a brow and waited.

Nic could sit here and stare his friend down, but he knew Robert was owed an explanation of sorts.

The problem was he didn't have one to give.

Not one that made sense, in any case.

"I've known Alison for a year now, and I've only ever seen her be unfailingly kind to people. She likes everyone," Rob continued. "She's worse than Abby for her good moods."

Nic couldn't help his grin as some of the old, unsociable monster inside his friend made itself known.

"Generally speaking, a good mood is considered a *good* thing," Nic drawled, momentarily distracted.

"I'm aware of that," Rob scowled. "It's just – a lot. A lot of singing and laughing and *flowers.*"

"We all know the flowers are your fault," Nic interjected. "It's terribly romantic, according to Abigail, Senna, and Amelia. So, you only have yourself to blame there."

Nic couldn't pretend to understand the significance of wildflowers when it came to Rob's marriage.

All he knew was that ever since Abigail had first arrived at Montvale Hall, it was constantly full of them, and Rob and Abigail were positively nauseating whenever it came up in conversation.

Even now, Rob's eyes were growing soft.

Nic didn't usually mind.

Today, it irritated him.

Another first.

And he was inclined to blame this on Alison Langton, too.

"Yes, well, be that as it may, I was a grumpy bastard for long enough that an abundance of gaiety still grates from time to time," Rob said now. "I'm just glad that Alison is determined to find herself a husband this Season. Then I'll only have one unashamedly happy blonde to deal with."

The feeling of – well, *something* unpleasant that shot through Nic at the mention of Alison Langton's future husband made him so uncomfortable he forced himself to ignore it.

"Two, if you count Lottie," Nic teased.

"Well, she got her mother's beauty, thank God," Rob answered. "But I'm hoping she gets at least some of her father's countenance."

Nic snorted in disbelief.

Robert doted on his wife. Everyone knew it. Nic knew nothing would make his friend happier than a daughter just like her mother in every way.

"Anyway, even if Lottie ends up as vivacious as her mother, that will still only leave me with two instead of three to take care of. It's already been a hard enough task keeping the dandies of Northumberland from my door. In the Marriage Mart, I haven't a hope in Hell of keeping them from battering the door down."

That unwelcome, uncomfortable feeling rose again inside Nic, and he finished his drink in one, great swallow before moving to refill his tumbler.

"You're going soft, then?" he asked with a lightness he didn't quite feel. "Losing your touch? I remember a time when people would be far too petrified to beat down the door of the Monster of Montvale."

Rob rolled his eyes at the moniker as he stepped forward to refill his own glass.

"We all know love makes heroes or fools of us all," he said. "A pretty face can drive a man to madness. And Alison's is prettier than most."

Prettier? If she were merely pretty, Nic wouldn't be having this problem.

She was beautiful. Earth-shatteringly, heartbreakingly so.

"She's determined to marry. And Abigail is determined to help her. Which means I've no choice but to let them come with their stupid posies and insipid poetry."

Rob shuddered, and Nic felt a spark of sympathy for his friend.

He could just imagine what they'd be like. For Rob spoke the truth. Someone that looked like Alison Langton and had connections to both the Duke of Montvale and the Marquess of Avondale would be fighting them off in droves.

If he could stand to be around the girl, he'd rather enjoy watching both Robert and James deal with them.

But for his sanity, he wouldn't be around any more than absolutely necessary.

"Anyway, I asked what was going on between the two of you outside."

"Nothing's going on," Nic answered quickly. "She clearly doesn't have a very high opinion of me. It happens." He shrugged.

"It doesn't happen," Rob answered. "Not to you. Nobody's ever said a negative word about you in all the years we've known each other."

If you don't count my father, Nic thought, though

he kept the sentiment to himself.

His friends knew nothing of his past with his father. Nor would they.

Speaking of the whole thing would only serve to make it real.

"Well, there's a first time for everything," he drawled with feigned nonchalance.

"And you don't like her either," Rob continued carefully.

Nic's navy eyes fled to Robert's.

"Why do you say that?" he asked, his heart thumping.

"I know you, Nic. I might not know what it is you do when you hide yourself away from one end of the day to the other. I might not know where you disappear to when Parliament finishes and Town empties of everyone except you. But I do know *you*. And you don't like her." He paused for a beat. "Why?"

Nic sighed, his head beginning to pound.

"I don't know, Rob," he answered finally. Truthfully. "She's spoilt. Far too pretty for her own good. Manipulative. You know she very nearly ruined things between Simon and Amelia?"

"Simon and Amelia nearly ruined things between Simon and Amelia," Rob countered. "And either one of them would tell you that themselves. Why, Amelia and Alison are the best of friends. And Simon doesn't even notice a woman who isn't his wife anymore."

Nic felt his frustration growing.

Why couldn't his friend see how bothersome Miss Langton was going to be?

Nic could just sense it in the chit. She was trouble.

"She might be spoilt, I'll grant you," Rob continued. "As spoilt as any of the Langton girls could be with the parents they had, in any case."

Nic frowned, wondering at that cryptic remark, but Rob wasn't finished.

"And she can't help what she looks like, Nic," he continued softly, just highlighting how insane Nic sounded for complaining about it. As though the girl were that beautiful on purpose to annoy him.

"I've just never seen you like this. And I wonder as to why."

Nic sighed once again.

"I already told you," he bit out, uncharacteristically snippy, bending his head and pinching the bridge of his nose. "I don't *know*."

He expected Robert to yell at him. Perhaps even threaten bodily harm for good measure.

But when there was nothing but silence, he looked back up to see his friend smiling enigmatically.

"I see," Rob said cryptically.

He saw? Nic laughed humourlessly to himself.

Whatever it was Rob saw, Nic didn't bloody see it. And he wouldn't ask what Robert meant because he suspected he wouldn't like the answer.

He was in for a long summer.

"WHY ARE YOU hiding from Nicholas?" Abigail asked for the hundredth time.

"I'm not hiding. From him or anyone," Alison answered for the hundredth time.

Abigail's stubbornness was infamous.

Alison's was worse.

And she would not be goaded into saying anything telling about the formidable duke.

It had been more than a little unfortunate getting caught saying such impolite things about him.

They weren't even true; that was the kicker.

Alison didn't find Lord Barnbury boring. If anything, it was quite the opposite. She was fascinated by him.

Why was he so sombre? Why was he single when he was almost ridiculously handsome? Why did he dislike her so?

It couldn't be because of what she'd said about him.

He had disliked her long before that.

From the moment they'd met in Dashford, she'd sensed his dislike coming off him in waves.

For someone who had always been treated well, spoiled even, by everyone she'd ever met, it had been quite disconcerting.

Every time she'd looked at him – and she had looked at him a *lot* – he'd been glowering.

And when she had tried to make conversation with him, he'd been blunt to the point of almost rudeness.

This wouldn't be such a concer for her if she didn't keep hearing from all corners about how polite and lovely and respectful the incomparable Duke of Barnbury was.

To everyone but her, apparently.

Alison had been so uncomfortable about it that she'd begged Robert to return to Montvale after Amelia's wedding to Lord Dashford.

They had meant to travel to London so Alison could get acquainted with the place before this year's Season.

But upon learning that the Duke of Barnbury never went home to Ireland and instead spent almost all his time in the capital, Alison had wanted to return to Montvale and hide herself away from the man.

She'd annoyed herself with the request, never having been the type to run away before. And as soon as they'd returned to Montvale, she'd felt utterly foolish.

Having spent the last year convincing herself that she'd misremembered how odd she'd felt in Lord Barnbury's presence, how affected she was by those navy-blue eyes and broad shoulders, his reappearance had come as something of a shock.

The scowl, however, hadn't. Nor had her unfortunate reaction to him.

She wanted to hate him as much as he clearly hated her.

Yet she'd watched him with Lottie, and her heart had flipped over at the sight of those big, strong arms holding her tiny niece.

Perhaps it was only because she'd been shamelessly watching him so closely, but Alison was sure she'd seen a flash of desolation in his eyes as he'd gazed at the precious bundle.

Though when he'd looked back up at Rob and Abby, pointedly *not* at Ally, he'd seemed once more coolly in control of himself.

She might have imagined it, she supposed.

According to everyone, his grace handled everyone and everything with perfect equanimity.

It seemed she was the only recipient of anything other than perfectly controlled politeness.

And inevitably, when Alison got a whiff of a challenge, she wanted to win.

Abigail was chattering away, talking about the invitations that had already arrived, the appointments she'd made with mantua makers and milliners and a plethora of other people needed to make Alison a success.

Alison was only half listening.

Her mind was churning with thoughts of the duke.

He seemed determined to dislike her, to avoid her.

And that made her determined to find out why.

She usually got what she wanted.

And, she decided, answers from the inscrutable duke would be no exception.

Chapter Five

"ARE THESE PARTIES always like this?"

Alison practically had to shout to her sister to be heard over the cacophony of sound in Lady Freeman's ballroom.

Her first social event, only a day after they'd arrived in London, was a veritable crush.

"It's because people have only just arrived in Town," Abigail assured her. "I would never usually pick such an event to attend because Lady Freeman has a terrible habit of inviting everything with a pulse. But we did want you to be seen, dear. And this is the best place for it."

Alison cast her gaze once more over the ever-growing crowd.

There were certainly plenty of people to be seen by.

She studied them all, her eyes colliding with more than one impudent stare.

The men in New York had been similarly forward, and she'd hated it then, too.

Judging by Robert's scowls and muffled oaths, he didn't particularly like it, either.

"Darling, why don't you go and see if Nic has arrived." Abigail smiled up at her husband.

Alison watched in envious fascination as Robert's expression went from murderous to adoring as he looked at his wife.

"I'm not going to leave you alone," he said, his hand reaching up to brush his knuckles along Abby's cheek.

It was an intimate moment, but Alison had long given up on feeling awkward around the pair.

They were like this together, always.

And they weren't the only ones.

James and Senna could barely keep their hands off each other, and Simon constantly looked as though he wanted to devour his wife on the spot.

Alison had always believed that English lords were reserved and cold, even prudish.

Yet Abigail's circle flew in the face of the strictures that Society tried to impose on husbands and wives.

They were all affectionate.

She knew Robert and Abigail didn't sleep in separate rooms and was certain none of the others did either.

The way James and Senna doted on Poppy was certainly not in keeping with traditional *ton* parents.

And as for Abby and Rob with Lottie – they had to be dragged away from the baby this evening and seemed to spend all their time adoring her.

Alison adored her, too, of course.

The very best part about coming to England had been staying with Abigail during her pregnancy then meeting little Lottie afterward.

And she'd grown close to Abby, too. Closer than they'd ever been at home under the disapproving, disinterested watch of their parents.

"I'm afraid to leave the two of you alone, lest the wolves descend," Robert said darkly, sending one such wolf scurrying with an infamous glower.

"And who amongst them would be brave enough to risk the ire of the Monster of Montvale?" Abigail quipped mischievously. "Truly, my love. If you do not leave, nobody will come near Alison. You'll frighten them all away."

"I don't see why that's necessarily a bad thing," Rob argued.

"Well, call me old fashioned, but I'd prefer if my sister got a chance to *speak* to a man before deciding on him as a husband."

Robert looked as though he would argue again, but then he sighed wearily.

"Fine. I'll go and see if Nic has arrived. Alison, please keep your wits about you."

Alison nodded dutifully, saving her smile for when her overprotective brother-in-law had already marched away.

"Honestly, what does he think I'll be foolish

enough to do?" she whispered to Abby as soon as the coast was clear.

"Who knows?" Abby shrugged. "Truthfully, he's barely spent more time in Society than you have. By the time I came to London for my Season, we were already betrothed. Before that, he wouldn't have been caught dead near Town unless he had business at Parliament. Last year, as you know, we spent more time at Dashford than London."

Abigail looked fondly after her retreating husband, who stood at least a head taller than almost every other man in the room.

She turned back to Alison.

"So, this is all rather new for him. I think he's secretly enjoying being a big brother."

Abigail's cornflower-blue eyes, so like Alison's own, darkened suddenly, and Alison remembered the tragic tale of Robert's sister's drowning.

Hating to see the sadness dull her sister's eyes, Alison reached out and plucked two glasses of champagne from a passing servant's tray.

"Then perhaps I should misbehave, just a little, so that he gets the full experience of being a fussy older brother?" She grinned.

Clinking her glass against Abby's, Alison laughed at her sister's expression of mischievous delight.

It was time to make an impression on London Society.

NICHOLAS SCOWLED ACROSS the ballroom; his mood darker than it had been in years.

Well, no, that wasn't strictly true.

In a year.

Since the last time the mere presence of Alison Langton had driven him mad, to be precise.

He had very nearly not come to the ball tonight. But he'd promised Rob, and Nicholas had never let anyone down in his life. Not since Ciara and their child.

He spent his entire life *not* letting people down. Or trying not to, at least.

And so, he'd armed himself with the reminder that he wasn't the type of man to get distracted by a pretty face or a smart mouth and entered the ballroom.

The second Nic had seen Alison Langton bedecked in white satin, looking for all the world like an angel, he'd felt that odd sensation he'd felt before stir to life inside him. A sensation he chose to ignore because, he reminded himself once again, he wasn't the type of man to be distracted by a pretty face or a smart mouth.

He'd been here a while and had yet to seek out his friend.

Instead he'd slipped in, refusing to be announced, wanting to avoid the inevitable fuss.

Being a duke, and a single one under the age of ninety at that, had its downsides.

Though Nic spent all his time now in London, futilely trying to assuage the guilt leftover from past mistakes, though he visited the worst, most depraved and treacherous pits of humanity London had to offer, nowhere was more dangerous to a single Peer with deep pockets than Town in the midst of the Marriage Mart.

Burying himself in a corner, as much as a man of over six feet could bury himself, Nic had allowed his navy-blue eyes to scan the ballroom.

It was a crush.

There were people everywhere.

Shrieks of laughter, shouts of greeting, and the valiant strains of an orchestra trying to be heard above the cacophony permeated the room.

And throughout it all, Nic's gaze searched for her.

And when he found her, his mood did not improve.

She was beautiful. Ethereal even. He knew it, and she knew it, too.

He watched while she laughed with her sister.

Watched as tongues began to hang out all around her, ignoring the red-hot anger that induced.

Nic never felt red-hot anger. He was careful not to feel too much of anything.

But he had to admit, to himself at least, that the

lascivious stares being sent Miss Langton's way were trying his patience more than most things did.

Suddenly, he spotted Rob cutting a path through the crowd toward him.

Nic couldn't contain his smile as the *haute monde* scurried out of the Monster of Montvale's way.

Rob couldn't be more different to the man he was before Abby, but he was even less fond of these things than Nic and could still pull out a scowl of displeasure to scare even the bravest of souls.

"You look as happy to be here as I feel," Nic said by way of greeting, as Rob shook his hand briefly then turned to take in the crowd.

"I used to think I'd have enjoyed taking Gina to London for her first Come Out," Rob said darkly by way of answer.

It was yet another testament to the change in the young duke that he would speak so freely of the sister whose death had made him the monster he'd been.

"But having to deal with the slobbering over Ally is proving that particular notion wrong. If I make it through the Season without shooting at least five of these little pups it will be a miracle."

Rob's sentiment matched Nic's own, though, of course, he couldn't confess such a thing.

Instead, he needed to do what he did best – be calm, reasonable, and sensible.

"You brought her here so that she could have a

Season," he reminded Rob gently. "This is exactly what you wanted. You must have known she'd be a sensation."

Rob muttered an oath under his breath.

"I knew," he sighed. "I'm not blind. But – well, look."

Nic didn't need to be asked twice.

He moved his eyes back to find Miss Langton was now surrounded by a veritable sea of gentlemen.

Once more, his anger attempted to flare. Once more, he ruthlessly tamped it down.

"You'll have your hands full, of that there is no doubt." His voice sounded strained even to his own ears.

Thankfully, Rob didn't seem to notice.

"We need to be careful here, Nic," Rob said, a touch desperately. "Ally is young. And, though I'm mightily fond of her, she's a little spoilt. According to Abby, of the three sisters, Alison was the only one who received any sort of affection from her mother. Though even that was fleeting. But she isn't used to having her behaviour reined in, and I fear that she's too naïve to understand the potential danger of certain men of the *ton*."

The description of Miss Langton was exactly what Nic suspected it would be; a spoilt Society princess who was used to people fawning over her.

Yet even as he scowled in her direction, he couldn't

help but notice the candlelight dance over her golden curls, or the sparkle in her cornflower eyes.

The way the angelic-looking white gown skimmed her body, making him feel anything but angelic.

This would not do. He could give Simon a run for his money in the inappropriate stakes if he allowed his thoughts to continue this way.

And that meant he needed to be as far away from the chit as was possible.

He dragged his thoughts and body back under his iron control and concentrated on his friend's words. Which is why he noticed Rob's use of the word 'we.'

"That sounds a lot like your problem, Rob, and nothing to do with me."

Robert glared at him.

"You cannot be serious," he said. "You know I can't keep an eye on her myself. Abby was a hoyden, Nic, and Alison makes her look like an angel. How can you expect me to deal with that, and a new baby?"

"If she behaves scandalously, you'll just ship her back to her father, no?"

"And suffer the wrath of my darling wife?" Rob asked wryly. "No, Alison wants her Season, and she'll get it. Vauxhall Gardens, ices at Gunther's, shopping on Bond Street, dancing at Almack's. She'll want to do it all, I'm sure. And you are going to help me."

Nic felt the beginnings of a headache behind his eyes.

"Rob, look at her."

They both looked back in the direction of Miss Langton.

If possible, it looked as though there were even more gentlemen clamouring for her attention now. And amongst them, some faces Nic would definitely *not* describe as gentlemen.

His fists clenched of their own accord.

"I hardly think you need my help in escorting the chit," he continued now, through gritted teeth. "She will hardly be short of company."

Rob sighed and turned back to face him, his face serious, his grey eyes imploring.

"That's exactly what I'm afraid of," he answered. "And that's exactly why I need you."

Chapter Six

T HE ENGLISH SEASON was exactly what Alison had imagined in would be.

Or at least Lady Freeman's ball was.

Her first foray into the *beau monde* of England was going very well.

She watched, pleased yet somewhat bemused, as four gentlemen dashed off to fetch some punch for her, whilst another tried to tell her some convoluted story about Tattersall's of all places, and yet more simply stared at her in a way that was less flattering than it was uncomfortable.

Abigail had been dragged off to speak to an acquaintance of the Dowager Duchess of Montvale, who wouldn't arrive until the month's end.

Robert had disappeared ages ago to play cards with the Duke of Barnbury.

Perhaps that was why Ally felt so on edge.

She was torn between wanting to be as far away from the stern duke as possible and wanting to throw herself into his path at every opportunity.

Though she should want to avoid him and his obvious dislike of her, the challenge he presented was too tempting. As was the need to know just *why* she annoyed him so.

She wasn't used to people just not liking her, though she did realise how unbearably smug that would sound if said aloud.

But more than that, as far as she knew, she'd given him no reason to feel that way about her.

From almost the first moment she'd met him in Lord Dashford's Liverpool manor, he'd been closed off, disapproving, and just not terribly nice.

It was disconcerting. Not least because much as he made it painfully obvious that he would never desire her company, Alison couldn't help herself from being drawn to the man.

Perhaps she was just plain shallow. After all, any-one with eyes could see how sinfully handsome he was with his navy-blue eyes, chestnut hair, rock solid muscles, and chiselled jaw.

Was she really so vacuous that she would dismiss everything about a man in favour of how well he looked?

All evening she had felt her gaze drawn around the room, searching for him.

Foolish in the extreme, given that he'd only bidden her the briefest of good evenings before rushing off.

Her dance card had been filled inordinately quick-ly, and though that both flattered and pleased her, she couldn't help but be disappointed that Lord Barnbury hadn't requested a set.

"Gentlemen, please excuse me. I simply must borrow my sister."

Abigail's timely interruption of Mr – Mr – oh, Mr. Somebody's description of good horseflesh couldn't have come at a better time.

With a general goodbye and a fluttering of her lashes, Alison hurried after her sister.

"Thank you," she sighed emphatically when they were out of earshot of the gentlemen. "I was full sure I'd fall asleep standing up listening to the correct way to buy a horse at Tattersall's!"

"Yes, well. I saw your eyes glaze over and thought I should come to the rescue. Who are you to dance the supper waltz with?" Abigail held out a gloved hand for Ally's dance card.

Alison duly handed it over.

"I haven't accepted any offers for the supper waltz," she replied. "After your dire warnings about displeasing the patronesses of Almack's, I thought it safer to wait until I'd received their permission to dance it."

That wasn't entirely true. The truth was she didn't really want to dance such an intimate dance with any of the men she'd met this evening.

She didn't want to dance it with anyone, really.

Anyone except the only man in the room who had no interest in her.

"Oh, I wouldn't worry overly much about that, dear," Abigail said now. "You are, after all, the sister-in-law of the Duke of Montvale. That gets you a certain amount of grace when it comes to these things."

Alison raised a sceptical brow.

"Then why all the warnings about it?"

"Well, we're American, Alison." Abigail shrugged. "And I have found that makes us a little less – *rigid* than our English counterparts. I might have overdone the sermons on propriety, truth be told. If James were here, our big cousin would make absolutely sure you didn't put a toe wrong. But I have never been exactly renowned for my demure nature, and Rob couldn't care less about the *ton* and its rules. So, I have been a little over-cautious, I'm sure."

"Oh, well." Alison patted her sister's hand. "No harm done. It is but one dance, and there isn't anyone I particularly wished to dance it with."

"No one at all?"

Alison opened her mouth to answer when a movement across the ballroom caught her eye.

He'd disappeared for a while, as had her brother-in-law. But there they stood – two handsome dukes, head and shoulders above almost everyone else in the room.

Robert was scowling, forboding and dangerous looking as always.

The only time Alison saw him look anything *other*

than slightly forboding was when he was looking at his wife or daughter.

And Poppy, too, when James's niece was around.

But Rob wasn't the one holding Ally's attention now.

No, her gaze was firmly fixed on his silent and stern companion.

Lord Barnbury's navy-blue eyes perused the ball-room. From here, Alison couldn't tell if he were pleased or displeased with what he saw.

His face was always a study in absolute stoicism, save for when he was frowning at her with obvious displeasure.

But his eyes always gave him away. Some tiny flicker of emotion always made itself known in his gaze.

It usually went unnoticed, she was sure. But then, she reasoned, it was unlikely that anyone other than her was looking closely enough to see.

Although, a quick glance around the room proved that wasn't necessarily the case.

Everywhere she looked there was a bevy of beautiful debutantes staring adoringly up at the formidable duke.

The only consolation was that he seemed oblivious to the lot of them.

Abigail coughed slightly, and Alison snapped her gaze back to her sister's identical one.

She realised she hadn't answered Abigail's question

but rather had gone mute whilst she'd studied every inch of Lord Barnbury and then eyed up the competition.

Competition! As though she had a chance of landing the stoic duke. As though she wanted to.

"So, no one?" Abigail repeated with a mischievous grin.

Alison felt her cheeks scald.

She refused to answer, choosing instead to sniff piously and look away.

Abigail's giggle did nothing to soothe Alison's embarrassment at having been caught gaping at a man who so clearly had no interest in her.

"Well, there aren't any gentlemen here with whom I would allow you to dance it, in any case," Abigail said casually. Casually enough to raise Alison's suspicions. "Except one."

"Oh?" Alison said, willing her cheeks to stop reddening. She could feel the heat rising in them again.

"Indeed," Abby said. "Nicholas," she continued, "He is a duke of equal standing to Robert and his oldest friend. There could be no impropriety in the action. And, of course, I know he can be trusted with you."

"Oh, yes. Because he dislikes me, so you wouldn't have to worry about any attempts at impropriety." Alison couldn't keep the slight bitterness from her tone.

Abigail's mouth opened in surprise.

"I was going to say it was because Nic is the steadiest, most dependable person I know," she said carefully. "Why do you think he dislikes you?"

Alison huffed out a breath, annoyed with herself for bringing it up.

"Oh, I think I made a rather poor first impression." She tried her best to sound *nonchalant*. There was certainly no way she would admit to having kissed the man and sent him running off without a word about it since. It was like he'd forgotten. Just to add insult to injury. "I think he was under the impression that I was trying to seduce Lord Dashford."

"Simon?" Abigail laughed. "Good Lord! How could he have thought that?"

"I don't know." Alison shrugged helplessly. "A misunderstanding? Though I got the impression that he didn't like me from the first moment we met."

"How strange." Abigail frowned. "I've never known Nic to dislike anyone. He's always been perfectly polite and kind to everyone."

"Well, how nice for me to be the first," Alison said dryly.

In truth, it stung a little to be the only person the duke apparently took a disliking to.

"Perhaps you are mistaken," Abigail said now, patting her hand reassuringly. "He can't have thought that Robert or James would have let Simon anywhere near you, in any case."

Alison laughed in spite of the uncomfortable conversation.

She knew that Lord Dashford had the well-earned title of Devil of Dashford for many years. The opposite of her cousin James in every possible way.

Yet when she had met Dashford, he'd already been completely besotted with Amelia.

So, though the stories of the earl's escapades shocked and scandalised her, she'd only ever known him as positively moon-eyed over the studious countess.

Yet the censure in Lord Barnbury's glare and tone on the brief occasions that he'd deigned to speak to her at Dashford, coupled with Amelia's mistaken belief that there was an affection between Alison and Simon, led Alison to believe that Lord Barnbury thought her nothing more than a flirtatious wanton.

And given he was so straight and *good,* she would be the worst type of person to someone like him.

"It's of no consequences, in any case," she said stoutly to her watchful sister. "He hasn't asked me to dance. Not the waltz. Not anything."

Abigail frowned once again.

"That's not like him," she said. "He must know that it would be expected of such a close friend to ask for a set. Besides, dancing with the Duke of Barnbury would do your reputation a world of good."

Abigail turned to stare across the ballroom at Lord

Barnbury whilst Alison felt steadily worse, before Abigail suddenly nodded her head.

"Right," Abigail tucked her arms through Alison's and began to pull her gently toward the gentlemen. "Come along."

"Wait, Abby. No!"

Alison tried to pull herself from her sister's grip without making a scene. But Abigail was stronger than she looked.

"I will not go over there begging for a dance, Abigail," Alison bit out, just loud enough for her sister to hear.

"Of course, you won't," Abigail responded airily. "A lady does not beg for a dance."

"Well, what are we doing then?"

"We're going to make *him* beg for a dance." She grinned.

Alison tried her best to look disapproving at Abigail's embarrassing plan.

But it was useless.

Her sister was determined and she, much to her shame, was secretly hoping that whatever Abigail planned to do would work.

Chapter Seven

"HELLO, SWEETHEART."

Alison stood awkwardly while Robert kissed Abby's hand then leaned forward to whisper in her ear.

She had no idea what he said, and judging from the blush on her sister's cheek, she didn't want to know.

She risked a glance at Lord Barnbury, but his face was a mask of indifference as he surveyed the room and avoided her eye.

Alison suddenly felt like going home and was about to suggest it, when Abigail pulled away from her husband and sighed dramatically.

"What's wrong?" Robert asked immediately.

"Oh, 'tis nothing," Abby said. "It's just been rather difficult keeping the gentlemen in check around Ally."

Alison frowned at her sister.

The men in the room had been attentive. Sometimes embarrassingly so. But it wasn't anything she felt she couldn't handle.

Robert muffled an oath, bizarrely glaring at Lord Barnbury, before turning his attention back to the ladies.

"I knew I shouldn't have left you alone," he said darkly. "Perhaps we should just go."

"We can't go," Abby said quickly before Alison had a chance to agree with her brother-in-law. "Why, Alison is promised for almost every dance. It would be just terrible for her prospects if she were to cry off now."

"Well then, tell me who was bothering her."

Alison felt rather alarmed at the dark expression on Robert's face, but Abby seemed unconcerned.

"It's not that anyone is bothering her per se." She sighed. "It's just there are so many of them. And I'm not sure all of their intentions are honourable."

This time, Robert's oath of annoyance was coupled by one from Lord Barnbury, and Alison's eyes flew to his face in time to see it darken with anger.

For a moment, he looked as terrifying as Robert, but just as quickly his expression cleared once more.

"Anyway, I'm sure it will be fine," Abby continued *nonchalantly*. "There is only the supper waltz free now, and as you know, whomever dances that with Alison will accompany her to dine, so she must choose wisely."

Alison was baffled by what her sister was up to.

She could only smile weakly at Robert's curious glance.

"Of course, I have cautioned against agreeing to

stand up with certain gentlemen but, well" – she turned to smile at Alison, patting her hand – "it's her first ball in England, and she cannot come to *too* much harm."

She paused in her little speech, and Alison saw a glint of mischief suddenly spark in her eyes.

"Even if she dances with Lord Tremont."

Alison gaped at Abigail.

Lord Tremont was one of the few people with whom she had been absolutely forbidden to dance. And as soon as she'd been introduced to the man, she'd guessed why.

His smile hadn't reached his cold, blue eyes and had put Alison in mind of a snake about to strike.

But before she could offer any sort of objection to Abigail's assertion, she was beaten to it by Robert and, to her surprise, Lord Barnbury.

"Over my dead body," Robert barked.

"She's not dancing with him," Lord Barnbury growled, and though Robert's objection was louder, Lord Barnbury's was the one that caught Alison's attention.

Surely, he didn't actually care with whom she danced?

"Oh dear." Abigail blinked wide, innocent eyes at the two gentlemen. "I didn't think your objections would be quite so strong."

"What are you thinking, Abby? You know of the

man's reputation."

Abigail frowned up at Lord Barnbury, looking for all the world like an innocently distressed miss.

Her sister could have had a marvellous career on the stage.

"I didn't think he could be quite so bad as people said. After all, Simon had the worst reputation of anyone I've ever known, and he's wonderful."

"Simon's reputation was of an incorrigible rake, and believe me, it was well deserved." Robert frowned. "But he was never cruel and never dangerous. The same cannot be said of that ba –"

"Be that as it may, she has already danced with everyone else who held her interest, isn't that right, dear?"

Alison managed to stutter incoherently, but it seemed enough for Abigail to plough on.

"And it really wouldn't do for her to dance *two* dances with the same gentleman at her first ball. So, what else is there to do? If she sits it out, he will only sit with her."

She smiled serenely at the two glowering dukes, and though Alison felt rather humiliated that her sister was trying to manipulate Lord Barnbury into dancing with her, she couldn't help but admire the tactic.

After a strained silence, Robert sighed.

"Fine," he snapped. "But I'll be keeping a close eye, and I swear if he tries to –"

"Miss Langton," Lord Barnbury interrupted whatever dire warning Robert was no doubt going to issue, and Alison looked up to see the handsome duke staring inscrutably at her. "Would you do me the honour of dancing the supper waltz with me?"

Alison's heart stopped dead in her chest before suddenly fluttering wildly.

It was foolish to feel excited about the poor man being forced to dance with her against his will.

Yet she couldn't help it.

No matter what her head told her, rather sternly, too, her heart wouldn't be reasoned with.

In a matter of moments, Lord Barnbury would be holding her in those strong arms of his.

Perhaps then she could get to the bottom of his antagonism toward her, and to the bottom of the mysterious attraction she felt toward him.

DAMN ABIGAIL FORSYTHE and her meddling.

Nicholas fought more than usual to keep his calm outward demeanour.

He guessed that Abigail had more sense than to let her sister near a blackguard like Tremont, but in the moment, he hadn't been able to think clearly.

He knew more about the depths of depravity that Peers like Tremont sank to than even his friends. He'd heard stories of them and seen them loiter around the brothels and hells of St. Giles enough to know there was truth in all the tales.

The idea of a creature like that putting his hands on Alison had made him lose all reason.

And before the mist of fury at the very idea of Fulham anywhere near Alison had subsided, he'd found himself asking her to dance.

The orchestra struck the chords he was at once hoping for and yet dreading, and he turned to offer his arm to the delectable blonde, telling himself repeatedly how one dance signified nothing.

How one girl wasn't much different to another.

The second she placed a delicate, gloved hand on his elbow, Nicholas knew he was wrong.

The jolt of desire that slammed into him nearly brought him to his knees.

He'd never felt the likes of it. And it terrified him.

Outwardly, he managed to remain poised and composed.

They reached the other dancers, and Nic took a deep breath before taking Miss Langton into his arms.

She was tiny. A slip of a girl.

Yet he could feel just how womanly she was when he placed his hand at her waist and drew her as close as he dare.

Preparing for impact, Nic finally looked down.

Just as he had feared, her cornflower eyes bored into him, making his mouth dry, his heart race, and his mind addled.

He'd expected an increase in the unwanted attraction he felt to her when he held her in his arms. Never could he have expected the sense of *rightness* at her being there.

He stared down at her, ensnared in her blue gaze.

Miss Langton didn't say a thing, merely gazed at him, trapping him in her spell.

The opening strains of the waltz reminded Nic to move.

It's just a dance, he told himself. *Like any other dance.*

And she's just a girl, he was sterner with himself in this point. *Like any other girl.*

Only as their bodies began to move, Miss Langton stepping closer, her hand searing his shoulder, her floral scent tormenting him, he knew that she wasn't like any other girl. And that was exactly the trouble.

"You are looking quite severe, your grace." She smiled up at him demurely, but her eyes were lit with that mischief he didn't trust. "Surely, I cannot have displeased you already. I haven't said anything outrageous, and I haven't trodden on your foot." She paused. "Not yet, in any case."

To his surprise, Nic felt a spark of humour, even a little entertainment at the chit, but he ruthlessly pushed it aside.

"You dance very well, Miss Langton," he said sombrely. "I cannot imagine that you would make the mistake of standing on my foot."

Her smile became positively wicked, and Nic felt that ever-present desire stir in response.

"I didn't say it would be a mistake."

She was incorrigible, and Nic felt his lips quirk in spite of himself.

"You would wish to do me bodily harm, Miss Langton? I can't imagine what I could have done to deserve such a thing."

Alison looked as surprised by Nic's flirtatious tone as he was to use it.

And when did I start thinking of her as Alison?

One evening in her company, one moment holding her in his arms, and he was suddenly thinking of her as Alison and holding her closer than was strictly appropriate, just to catch the maddening scent of her skin, just to wrap his hand a little more firmly around her delicate waist.

"Given that your favourite thing in the world seems to be scolding me, I'm sure it won't be long before I find a good reason," she answered frankly and with an honesty he couldn't help but admire.

Nic felt both a twinge of guilt and a twinge of something infinitely more dangerous.

He couldn't think of a thing to say in response, so he said nothing at all. Instead, he enjoyed the excruciating pleasure of having her in his arms.

Chapter Eight

THE DAY DAWNED bright and golden, and Alison lay in bed listening to the sounds of her brother-in-law's household awakening.

Though she had barely slept a wink last night, she was still awake with the lark.

Last night's ball had been one of the most wonderful evenings of her life.

She had enjoyed it immensely.

She had been introduced to all the right people, met friends of Abigail and Robert, been lavished with attention by gentlemen whose names she couldn't even remember.

But none of it could come close to the elation of dancing with Lord Barnbury.

Even now, after a restless night thinking of him and fitful sleep dreaming of him, Alison's heart raced with excitement.

The feeling of being in his arms, the strength of him even as he held her, as though she were made of the finest china. The scent of him, masculine and intoxicating surrounding her – and miraculously, the smile, brief though it was, making his navy-blue eyes brighter.

All of it made Alison positively dizzy with excitement, and desire, and so many wonderful new emotions that she could barely keep control of them.

And even though he'd ended their dance in his usual stoic fashion, even though he'd been once again subdued whilst they'd eaten supper with Abigail and Robert, it mattered not to Alison.

She'd seen a brief, tantalising glimpse of a sense of humour beneath the serious exterior, and it made her determined to bring it out in him again.

Feeling giddy with anticipation and something that it was far too soon to even be contemplating about the dutiful duke, Alison rang the bell for her maid.

As soon as Eliza came in with a cup of chocolate, Alison leapt from the bed.

She had no idea what Abigail had planned for today, but she dearly hoped it included seeing Lord Barnbury again.

"What would you like to wear for afternoon calls, Miss Langton? The duchess is to host an *At Home*, so you'll be wanting something to impress your suitors."

Alison grinned at the outspoken maid. Eliza had come over from the Americas with Alison, and she was so glad to have her own maid with her. She knew it had been a sacrifice for Eliza to leave behind her family to come here.

More than it had been for Alison.

She'd barely gotten a goodbye from anyone except Beth. And Beth was the only one she really, truly missed.

"You assume that I'll have suitors," she laughed. "What if everyone hated me?"

"Tosh," her maid responded immediately. "They'll be hammering the door down, Miss. Now, how about the blue?"

She pulled out an exquisite day dress in the palest shade of sky-blue. When the mantua maker that Robert had summoned to Montvale Hall had delivered the dress before their journey to London, Alison had fallen in love with it.

It was simple in its cut, unadorned save for white piping along the sweetheart neckline, but the colour made her eyes seem bluer and hair brighter.

"It's perfect." She nodded her approval as she sipped her chocolate.

"Well then, let's get you ready for all those gentlemen coming to call," Eliza said as she swept from the room to press the gown.

Alison moved to the window of her bedchamber, looking out at the verdant grass and colourful flowerbeds of Abigail's gardens.

She didn't know if there would be as many gentlemen calling as Eliza imagined, but it was of no matter. She was only interested in one.

"Your grace, 'tis good to see you."

Nicholas was pulled from his distracted reverie by the sound of a voice calling to him, the distinctive Irish brogue filling his ears.

He turned to smile at the plump, aproned woman bustling toward him.

Mrs. Cafferty was a gem. Someone he trusted with his life and with this centre, which was so important to him.

There wasn't much to smile about in St. Giles, this part in particular, yet the middle-aged, portly house-keeper seemed perpetually cheery.

"How do you do, Mrs. Cafferty?" Nic bowed to the woman as though she were a duchess.

She might not have a title, but she most certainly had his respect.

"I could complain, your grace, but sure who'd listen?" She smiled, her faded green eyes crinkling at the corners. "We weren't expecting you till week's end, your grace. I hope nothing is amiss?"

"No, indeed. Everything is running smoothly as ever, I'm sure. I was just of a mind to drop in, if it's not an imposition?"

"Tsk. An imposition! How could you be imposing in your own building, your grace? Come along then."

Being a duke, only a step down from royalty, Nic wasn't ordered about the place by anyone. Yet here in the Rookery, when Mrs. Cafferty told him to come along, he made haste to follow the redoubtable lady.

Nic had first met the flame-haired woman ten years prior when he'd been searching like a man possessed for Ciara and their unborn babe.

Though Mrs. Cafferty's ginger curls were now streaked with grey, she was much the same as she had been back then; taking care of everyone around her, working her fingers to the bone to ensure those under her wing were as safe and well as they could be in the slums of St. Giles, and determined to make the world a better, safer place for the children she took care of in whatever way she could.

He'd come across Mrs. Cafferty and her brood of unknown, unwanted children when he'd first entered the hell of the intricate, never-ending streets of Little Ireland.

She had been suspicious of him at first, knowing first-hand just what it could mean when a Peer came searching for children on this side of London.

Nicholas couldn't even stomach the briefest thought on it.

But she'd trusted him and thankfully believed that his intentions were good.

More than that, Mrs. Cafferty had been the one to whom he'd turned for comfort when he'd finally discovered the truth about Ciara. Had been there with him the day he'd been forced to say goodbye to the dream of finding his babe forever.

She had become something of a mother figure to Nic, since he never saw his own anymore.

The occasional letter was all the correspondence he had with the duchess. And it was all he wanted. Even his sisters, both married with families of their own, were on the peripheral of Nic's life.

Though they'd been young when his father had acted so abominably, and held no blame for what had befallen Ciara and the baby, Nic still kept them at a distance. He'd seen them right, given them dowries and ensured they were were well taken care of during their respective Come Outs. But since they'd both made good matches and settled down, Nic had little to do with them. Not because he didn't care. Because he didn't know how to be close to them without being reminded of his parents.

Whilst his mother hadn't been quite as cruel as his father, she was cut from the same cloth and had been just as eager to get rid of Ciara as the old duke had.

Nic and Mrs. Cafferty were now travelling down the hallway of one of the buildings Nic had procured on the outskirts of Little Ireland.

After he'd learned of the fate of Ciara, Nic had dedicated his time to trying to win the unwinnable war against poverty, crime, and depravity in the streets of

St. Giles.

He never would. He knew that.

But he would keep on trying.

One of his first attempts at salving his conscience had been this building – a home of sorts for the children of the Rookery. Somewhere they would have full bellies and a clean place to sleep. Somewhere safe from the monsters that lurked on these streets. Monsters like the one who'd killed Ciara and his child.

Before his mind could drag him down into his bleak memories, Mrs. Cafferty once more pulled him from his thoughts.

"The children will be only delighted to see you again, your grace." She was sounding a little breathless as they'd now begun the ascent to her office on the second floor of the three-storey building, but Nic knew better than to mention it. "Their letters and numbers are coming along wonderfully."

"And the new arrivals?" he asked quietly.

Only two weeks ago, Nic had caught a brother and sister trying to steal his coin. A few questions answered not by the mutinous, hard-edged boy of ten but by his skinny, haunted-looking sister of only six told him what he'd already suspected. They were alone in this world. Their mother had died only two years before and since neither knew who their father was, or if they even had the same father, there was nobody to help them.

It had taken some convincing, but finally Nic managed to get them to come to Mrs. Cafferty's, as the place was affectionately known.

"John and his sister. She was never named," Mrs. Cafferty said stoutly, but Nic knew that knowledge would hurt the woman as much as it hurt him to hear it. "We've taken to calling her Bonnie, since she's such a pretty little thing. They're settling in as well as can be expected," the Irishwoman said now. "It's a big adjustment, going from life on the streets to a home. They still have the look of children who are expecting the worst," she said softly. "But sure, time will prove their safety like nothing else."

By now they had reached the corridor that housed Mrs. Cafferty's modest rooms, along with a schoolroom, rooms kept for when the doctor visited, and a playroom. Above stairs was where the children and the rest of the staff slept.

The door of the playroom was opened and as they passed, Nic caught sight of the new arrivals.

The boy, John, looked briefly up at Nic but dropped his gaze almost immediately, staring defiantly at the toy soldiers in front of him.

Whilst he was wondering if he should try to speak to the child, he felt a tug on his fawn breeches.

Looking down, Nic felt his heart slam nearly out of his chest as he looked into the face of the little girl he'd saved.

Mrs. Cafferty was right. She was a bonnie little thing. Her name suited her.

But it wasn't that which had Nic's heart hammering.

It was the golden curls. The huge blue eyes. The shy but impish smile.

She looked like Poppy, he thought. But more than that – she looked like Alison Langton.

And just like that, all his best laid plans – to come here and distract himself with the work he loved to do, with the people he needed to help – went completely awry.

Alison Langton had been lurking on the periphery of his thoughts, just waiting for him to slip up so she could fill every part of his mind.

Now, as he stood there looking at the beautiful child, shying from the images and possibilities she presented him with, he couldn't help but think of Alison.

Outwardly he was his usual self, and he bent to speak softly to the child, conscious of her brother watching closely from the corner.

But inside, a veritable storm was rattling around inside him.

A golden-haired, blue-eyed storm. One he wasn't sure he'd survive.

Chapter Nine

"O F ALL THE jewels London may have to offer, Miss Langton, you are truly the best of them."

Alison gritted her teeth as Lord Fulham ran a somewhat insolent gaze over her.

When the butler had announced Lord Fulham, Alison had half expected Robert to refuse the man entry. However, a hastily whispered warning from Abigail not to create a scene in front of their other visitors meant Robert had allowed it, albeit reluctantly.

He was handsome, of that there was no doubt. Tall and slim, his blonde hair was styled in the Brutus cut that was all the rage.

Lord Barnbury's hair was chestnut, she thought, and longer than the severity of Fulham's.

Lord Fulham's eyes were a pale, icy blue. Nicholas's were a deep, warm navy.

Get a hold of yourself, Alison, she scolded herself. But it was no use.

Yes, he was handsome, if a little slimy. And he was being almost obscenely attentive. Yet she couldn't stop her mind from wandering to her disinterested duke.

It had been a week since she had danced with the duke at the ball. The man had since disappeared. All afternoon she'd watched the door. As she had done every afternoon.

Abigail had declared Alison a sensation, and it had been necessary for them to be "at home" for the entire week in order for Alison to be available to speak to her many admirers.

She was more than a little flattered that so many people had taken an interest in her.

Yet every time the butler knocked, with yet another card upon a silver platter, her heart raced then sank to her toes.

It was never the Duke of Barnbury. No matter how much she wished it to be.

Eliza had been right, in any case, when she'd predicted that Alison would be in demand.

At any given moment the drawing room, which was by no means small, was full to the brim with people.

Though there were a smattering of ladies present, there was an abundance of men. Men who brought posies of beautiful flowers and lavished her with attention and compliments.

It was far less enjoyable than she would have imagined.

Yet every time she looked over at Abigail, her sister smiled broadly, like a proud mama. And it reminded

Alison of the effort and money Abigail and Robert were expending to give her this Season.

So, she decided she needed to get her mind away from apathetic duke and focus on one of the many gentlemen here who wanted her company. Even sought her company, as opposed to it being forced upon them.

She looked briefly to her brother-in-law, who was standing by the fireplace, a scowl upon his face.

Nobody in the room seemed brave enough to go near him, and he didn't seem to mind.

That was another thing – if she hurried up and chose a husband, Robert would get his life of solitude back.

He could take Lottie and Abby back to Northumberland where he was happy and comfortable.

Alison's stomach twisted painfully as she thought of marrying and moving away from Abigail and Robert.

But that's what she'd come here for.

If she could leave an ocean between herself and her parents and younger sister, she could leave a few counties between herself and her older sister, surely.

With a renewed sense of purpose, Alison turned her full attention to Lord Fulham.

"Do you enjoy the theatre, Miss Langton?" he asked now, his eyes slowly perusing her body in a way that made her want to cover herself in a shawl.

Her simple, lemon muslin was anything but vulgar, yet Lord Fulham made her feel as though she were some sort of lightskirt.

But perhaps she had been focusing so much on disdainful, cold stares that she was misconstruing friendly appreciation.

"I do, my lord." She smiled. "In fact, I believe we are to attend this evening's performance."

"Ah," he smiled. "I had hoped to invite to you attend with me."

Alison froze, wondering what the etiquette was in this situation.

Should she invite Lord Fulham to join them in Robert's box? That didn't seem proper, yet he wasn't speaking, so she was under the distinct impression that he was expecting *something*.

They had the room.

Robert would be escorting both Abigail and herself that evening, so it wasn't as though Lord Fulham wouldn't have a space. And truth be told, she'd far rather be escorted by a gentleman of her own than be taken out by her brother-in-law.

"W-well, my lord – if his grace doesn't mind, I –"

"His grace, the Duke of Barnbury, your grace."

Alison's head whipped around at the sound of the butler's sudden announcement, and there he was, filling the doorway looking almost absurdly handsome in a dark green superfine, fawn breeches, and shiny

Hessians.

His eyes travelled around the room and its occupants, all of them scrambling to bow and curtsey, before landing on Alison.

Her breath caught at the brief flare of some intense emotion in his eyes before they became as impassive as always.

He frowned as his gaze travelled from her to Lord Fulham and back again.

Alison smiled tentatively.

When he didn't return the gesture, rather turned to speak to Robert, who had approached him, her temper and an imp of mischief awakened.

"Lord Barnbury doesn't look too pleased with what he sees," Fulham said evenly. Alison noticed that he was watching her closely.

"Is he ever?" she asked dryly, earning a laugh.

"Touché, my dear. In all the years I've known him, I don't think I've ever seen him smile."

Alison's heart twisted a little to be engaging in such vulgar conversation about the duke, but when she looked his way again, she saw he was managing to smile quite well at the few ladies in the room who had closed in on him.

The jealousy she felt was surprising in its intensity.

"I'd say that perhaps the bad moods come from losing at the tables in his favourite haunts, but the man is rich as Croesus, so it can't be that."

This caught Alison's attention when it had been once more wandering across the room, and she frowned in confusion at Lord Fulham.

"Lord Barnbury is a gamer?" she asked.

Alison was surprised to hear it. He didn't seem the type.

She knew he played cards at parties and with Robert, James, and Lord Dashford. But gambling in hells? It was surprising.

"I assume so. He and I do not frequent the same places, but I see him around St. Giles all the time. There are only two reasons a man would be in that part of London, Miss Langton. And I won't offend your sensibilities by telling you about the other one."

Alison felt a blush heat her cheeks at Lord Fulham's outrageous comment. She knew exactly what he was implying and though she didn't consider herself a prude, it made her feel vaguely uncomfortable.

She wouldn't, however, act like an unsophisticated little girl, so she laughed delicately.

"I'm quite sure I understand your meaning, Lord Fulham. I'm surprised to hear that his grace is interested in either of those things, to be frank."

"He seems far too stuffy, I grant you." Lord Fulham leaned forward to whisper conspiratorially. He smelt rather pleasant. "But I see him around St. Giles enough to know that he frequents the place. What other reason could there be?"

That wasn't at all in keeping with the impression Alison had formed of him.

In truth, rather than finding it off-putting, she found this titbit of information rather exciting.

She didn't know St. Giles. Nor would she, if Robert and James had anything to do with it.

According to her over-protective relatives, it wasn't even safe to be *near* that part of London, let alone in it.

So why would someone as safe and dutiful as the Duke of Barnbury frequent it so often?

Alison turned to study the duke once more, and her breath caught when she realised he was already studying her.

Well, she wasn't going to smile at the blighter again, just for him to scowl at her.

Though her heart hammered in response to whatever stormy emotion was darkening his navy eyes, she turned her head and ignored him.

"Lord Fulham, I'm sure my brother-in-law and sister would be happy to have you join us in the Montvale box at the theatre this evening."

It was bold.

Probably scandalous in this world of virtue and judgment.

But she wanted to spend the evening with a man who wanted her company, instead of thinking about a man who could barely tolerate it.

Lord Fulham's smile was triumphant.

"I would be honoured. Thank you, Miss Langton."

He took his leave and almost immediately, his place was filled by yet another gentleman, with yet another bouquet of flowers.

Alison tried not to find the entire thing tedious.

She risked a glance once more at Lord Barnbury.

He had left. And hadn't said goodbye. Hadn't even said hello, for that matter.

Alison ignored the dip of disappointment in her stomach and instead settled in to listen to whatever nonsense she was about to be privy to.

Chapter Ten

WHAT THE BLOODY hell was he doing here?

Nic berated himself, not for the first time, as he watched the hordes of people in and around the entrance of the theatre.

As with most *ton* events, he didn't particularly like or dislike them. He attended. He was cordial. He spent time with whichever of his friends and acquaintances were there, and then he went home feeling no worse and no better.

This evening, however, he was on edge.

He watched everyone closely, searching against his will for a glimpse of golden hair, or impossibly bright blue eyes, or a smile that looked like pure devilment.

Earlier, he'd heard Alison Langton invite that cretin Fulham to join her at the theatre.

She obviously hadn't checked with Rob or Abby if this would be acceptable, because there was no way in Hell Rob would let someone like Fulham near Alison.

It was none of Nic's business, of course. Yet here he found himself, at the opening night of a play he had no interest in, standing like a damned watchdog waiting to protect a lady who he wasn't even sure he particularly liked.

If his friends could see him now, or at least see the emotions roiling inside him that he was so careful to keep hidden below the surface, he'd never live it down.

Going to Rob's house that afternoon had been a mistake.

Coming here this evening was a mistake.

His famous self-control was slipping by the day, and he had no idea what to do about it.

He'd managed to spend an entire week away from Alison Langton and all the temptation she presented. Why did his resolve have to crack today of all days, so he felt compelled to act as a chaperone for the girl?

The worst part was that he'd rushed over here, hell-bent on keeping an eye on Alison and Fulham, and hadn't given a thought as to who he would sit with or what he would do.

Though he put little store in the opinion of the *beau monde*, even he knew that sitting alone in his box would be – odd.

He would, of course, be welcome to sit in Robert's box, but that meant sitting between Rob and Abby, and Fulham and Alison.

That didn't exactly appeal, either.

Although he would be close enough to wring Fulham's neck if he acted anything other than the perfect gentleman.

Damn it. This was a mistake.

Nic was just admitting defeat to himself and turning to slip quietly away, when he heard a familiar voice.

"Crack a smile, Saint Nic, or a dog might mistake you for one of these statues and pi– oof."

Nic turned around in time to see Lady Dashford give her husband a quick elbow to the ribs, stopping his scandalous statement before he could finish it.

Nic smiled his first real smile in days as he stepped forward to kiss Amelia's cheek and shake Simon's hand.

"The wanderers return." He grinned, his eyes taking in one of his oldest friends, not quite believing the change in him.

Simon looked as he ever did, jet-black hair, brown, almost black eyes. But his countenance was different.

No longer dissolute and displeased with everything he saw, no longer dangerous and debauched.

The former Devil of Dashford looked – content. That was it. Truly happy.

And for the first time in a long time, Nic felt a knife of jealousy stab at him.

He was happy for his friend, of course. The devil and his bluestocking bride belonged together. They were perfect for each other.

And Nic was as pleased for Simon as he had been for James when he'd married Senna, and Rob when he'd married Abby.

But never before had he felt the ugliness of jealousy mar his happiness.

So, why now?

"Why are you out here alone?" Simon asked.

Nic would rather walk over hot coals than admit he'd been watching for the arrival of Miss Langton.

"I was waiting to hear about all of your wonderful adventures, of course," he said equably.

Simon's frown said the earl knew he was lying, but just as Nic had hoped, the mention of the couple's travels through Europe was enough to set the history loving Amelia off, and she launched into a detailed description of every archaeological site they'd visited and what she'd discovered there.

Nic listened politely to the lady's chatter. Amelia was as bright as she was beautiful, and her marriage to the devilish earl had changed her, too.

Gone was the shy wallflower who used to sit in corners and mumble to herself.

In her place was a regal, confident countess be-decked in satin and diamonds and taking the attention she was garnering in her stride.

The news of the debauched Devil of Dashford's marriage had caused nothing short of an uproar amongst the *ton*. And given that Simon and Amelia had hightailed it off to Scotland as soon as they'd married, then on to Norway, then Italy, nobody had gotten the chance to really ogle the pair until now, and by the sounds of the whispers and looks of raised eyebrows, the *ton* were taking full advantage now.

"You are quite the sensation," Nic said wryly when Amelia paused for a breath.

She frowned slightly, her spectacles slipping down her nose.

"Odd creatures," she said matter-of-factly, before shrugging and turning back to Nic.

"Tell me, how does Alison get on?" she asked now, and Nic tensed immediately. Foolish but true.

"I have no idea," Nic answered as evenly as he could. "I have seen her but rarely."

"You haven't seen her?" Simon asked, his shock evident in his tone.

"I have, of course. A bit." Nic scrambled for equanimity, hating the speculative gleam in Simon's eyes. "But I've been busy, and –"

"Amelia!"

An excited cry rent the air, saving Nic from answering, and they all turned to see Miss Langton bounding up the steps, unaware or uncaring about the sensation she was causing.

Amelia seemed as unconcerned in what people thought as Alison was, and she rushed to meet her friend halfway.

Simon and Nic watched as the ladies threw their arms around each other, Nic desperately trying not to be jealous of the countess.

"So," Simon said casually. Too casually.

"So?"

"Do you want to tell me what's going on?"

Nic swallowed hard.

"I don't know what you mean," he said.

The silence was deafening, but he refused to break it, just as he refused to look at his friend. He couldn't have anyway, even if he'd wished to. For at that moment, Alison was joined by Lord Fulham, who placed a proprietary hand on her lower back.

Nic muffled a black oath as he took in the scene.

"Nicholas Fyfe, as I live and breathe, I never thought I'd see the day."

Nic turned to scowl at Simon, his anger flaring at his friend's delighted look.

"Shut up, Simon," he said, uncharacteristically irritable.

This just served to amuse Simon more, and he chuckled softly.

"Go to Hell, Simon," Nicholas bit out.

"Been there, my friend," Simon laughed. "Until Amelia. And it would appear that you've taken my place."

ALISON WAS TRYING to pay attention to the performance on stage, yet there were far too many distracting things going on around her.

For one thing, Lord Fulham seemed to brush against her an inordinate amount of times.

And from the growls emanating from Robert, she wasn't the only one to notice.

She told herself to feel flattered by Lord Fulham's attentions. He was a handsome, wealthy Peer. And whilst Robert had rung a peal over her head when he'd found out that she'd invited him to the theatre that night, Alison was sure he wasn't that bad.

It had only been Alison begging Abigail, and Abigail subsequently doing whatever it was she did to make Robert agree to things that led to Lord Fulham accompanying them.

This vaguely uncomfortable feeling Alison got when he sat a little too close, or his hand brushed the exposed skin between her short-sleeved pink evening gown, and white satin glove, was just her inexperience and nothing more.

Besides, even Lord Fulham's attentions couldn't quite hold her focus.

Not when Robert's box was directly across from Lord Dashford's.

Not when she could see Lord Barnbury from where she sat.

Throughout the entire first half of the performance, though she made a valiant effort to concentrate on the actors, or on Lord Fulham's comments, Alison's gaze was repeatedly drawn over to the Dashford box and the navy-eyed duke within.

And every time she looked over, her stomach fluttered wildly.

Because he was watching her.

Neither smiling nor frowning, at least from what she could tell at this distance.

Alison had no idea if he were pleased or displeased.

All she knew was that he was watching.

And though she didn't want it to, that fact made her heart sing.

By the intermission of the play, Alison couldn't have said what theatre they were in let alone what performance they were watching.

All around them, people were shuffling about, either to partake in refreshments or visit each other's boxes.

"My dear Miss Langton, allow me to fetch you some ratafia."

Alison smiled graciously at Lord Fulham's attentiveness.

When he left, she felt her shoulders sag in relief.

That probably wasn't supposed to happen during a courtship.

"What did you think of the performance, Ally?" Abigail asked.

"Oh, er –" She didn't know what to say. She hadn't seen any of it! "I-I'm not sure."

"Hmm. Perhaps that's because you paid no attention to it." Abigail grinned.

Alison felt her cheeks heat.

"I might have been a little distracted," she finally admitted.

"And what distracted you? Lord Fulham's attentions, or –"

Abigail was interrupted by the sudden arrival of Lord Barnbury, Lord Dashford, and Amelia.

Before any of them could issue a greeting, Lord Barnbury whirled around to face Robert.

"What are you about, letting that blackguard paw at her in full view of the theatre?"

There was a shocked silence in the face of Lord Barnbury's furious outburst as all eyes stared at the man who had never before lost his composure.

"What the hell do you mean?" Robert finally snapped, his temper obviously flaring in the face of Lord Barnbury's criticism.

"I mean, why weren't you bloody well watching her?" Lord Barnbury snapped back.

Alison jumped to her feet, feeling guilty and uncomfortable that the two old friends were arguing. About *her.*

"Don't be so ridiculous," Robert spat. "How much danger do you think she could have been in, in a theatre box?"

"I don't know," Lord Dashford interrupted, most

unhelpfully. "I was able to do an obscene amount of damage in a theatre box. In fact –"

"That's not helpful, Simon," Abigail interrupted whatever salacious thing Lord Dashford was about to say.

"Right, carry on." He grinned unrepentantly.

"You need to do a better job watching her," Lord Barnbury said now.

Alison was getting mightily sick of them talking about her as though she weren't there.

"Robert, Lord Fulham was not behaving untowardly," she spoke up. "I –"

Suddenly, Lord Barnbury rounded on her.

"Perhaps in America it is acceptable for single ladies to act in such a manner, Miss Langton," he bit out. "But in England, we tend to have standards about these things."

Alison heard gasps of shock all around her, but her focus remained on the pompous, overbearing, stuffy man in front of her.

"Perhaps in England it is acceptable for arrogant, self-important, boring old men to tell young ladies how they should behave. But in America, we tend not to pay them any mind. A custom that I think will serve me very well on this side of the ocean."

Without awaiting a response from Lord Barnbury or from anyone else, Alison turned on her heel and dashed from the box.

She didn't want to speak to anyone.

She didn't want to see Lord Fulham again after the horrid things Lord Barnbury had said.

More than anything, she never wanted to see or speak to that odious duke again.

Chapter Eleven

"THAT WAS QUITE a night last night."

Alison looked up with a grimace as Abigail swept into the morning room, resplendent in a seafoam day dress.

Alison hadn't been able to sleep much and when the birds began to sing as dawn broke, she had given up and come downstairs.

The servants had only been starting their chores, so she had wandered around listlessly getting in everyone's way.

The truth was that she found the mornings a tad boring.

When Lottie was up, it was marvellous. She could play all day with her golden-haired niece.

But Lottie was still abed, as were Robert and Abigail. And so, she'd wandered aimlessly around the house, for the first time missing home.

At home she would have her friends. People she had known since finishing school, on whom she could call without the strictures of polite Society.

She would have her horse, and the space to ride it

however long she wanted.

She would have her charity work, too. Something that she missed greatly.

It was a source of some embarrassment for Mrs. Langton that Alison had involved herself so heavily with the orphanage that Mama had patronised.

Whilst Mama had told them it was expected for a lady of good breeding to be on the board of some charities, she was loathe to have her daughters actually go near the places.

But Alison hadn't cared. She had visited the orphanage, and the hospital for wounded soldiers, and spent hours reading to the men and teaching the children to read and sing and do all sorts of things.

Here, she wouldn't even know where to begin.

At Montvale, she had helped Abigail with her duties as duchess, but the truth was that Montvale and its surroundings were thriving, as were all of Robert's holdings. His tenants were very well looked after. And the children were provided with a school and an excellent tutor.

Alison hadn't been much use. And here in London, she was even less useful.

She'd breakfasted on tea and toast, lost in her maudlin thoughts, which is how Abigail found her now.

"I'm sorry for my behaviour, Abby," she said, her cheeks flushing with shame at her actions the previous night. "I allowed my temper to get the better of me, and I made you and Robert leave early. I didn't even bid Lord Fulham farewell. I behaved dreadfully."

She studied the pattern on her cup, refusing to meet what was sure to be censorious gaze.

When her apology was met with silence, however, Alison couldn't bear it any longer and risked a glance at her sister.

Abigail, rather than looking ashamed, or furious, was smiling kindly.

"You know, I have never in my life seen Nicholas anything other than completely calm and collected. It was quite a shock, to see him so overset."

Mention of the overbearing duke immediately awoke Alison's temper.

"You've mentioned that before," she said bitterly. "I've only ever known him to be an unbearable, insufferable bore."

Abigail's eyes widened and bizarrely, she looked as though she were trying to hide a smile.

"Yes, I've noticed. It's certainly strange."

Alison squinted suspiciously at her older sister, but Abigail just stared innocently back.

Before she could question her sister's antics however, the door to the morning room opened and Robert swept in carrying Lottie in his arms.

He walked straight over to Abigail and placed a gentle kiss on her lips. Though it was brief and not at all inappropriate, there was such a feeling of love between the two of them that Alison felt as though she were encroaching on a private moment.

And she wanted the same thing. So very desperately.

She knew Robert credited Abigail with saving him from a life filled with pain and despair.

The drowning of his younger sister when he, James, Simon, and Nicholas were children had affected them all. But none more so than Robert, who had tried and failed to save her.

Abigail loved to tease Robert about how mean he had been to her when they'd first met. And though Robert didn't deny it, Alison found it hard to believe.

He adored his wife, and, unlike other Peers, he wasn't afraid or ashamed to show it.

Abigail held out her arms for the baby, and Robert handed her over before moving to take his seat at the head of the table.

"Robert, I wanted to apologise for my outburst last night." Alison jumped straight into her apology, wanting to get it over with. "I never meant to cause a scene, and I feel just awful that you and your friend argued because of me."

"We didn't argue because of you, Ally." Robert smiled kindly. "We argued because Nic is losing his mind. It's really quite entertaining."

Alison frowned in confusion.

She was relieved that Robert wasn't cross with her, but his cryptic remarks, along with Abigail's, only served to confuse her.

Talk turned to Charlotte, to their upcoming attendance at Almack's, to Alison's visit to the mantua maker. But Alison barely joined in.

She was feeling unsettled. Even a little listless.

Here she had London at her feet. Handsome gentlemen like Lord Fulham dancing attendance on her. Vouchers to Almack's and invitations to every possible social event.

She should be happy. Excited and anticipating all the marvellous things she would experience.

Once again, she had allowed the Duke of Barnbury and his obvious disdain affect her far more than he should be allowed to.

"So, Ally. Shopping in an hour?"

Abigail's question interrupted Alison's maudlin thoughts.

She gave her sister the brightest smile she could manage.

"Wonderful," she said.

And it would be. She would make sure of it.

If Lord Barnbury wanted to accuse her of being shallow and frivolous, then she would show him just how frivolous she could be.

"WHAT'S ALL THIS I hear about you actually showing some emotion last night? And in public, too."

Nicholas looked up from his tumbler of brandy to see James Harrington, Marquess of Avondale grinning down at him.

Alison's cousin.

With the same blonde hair and blue eyes.

Marvellous.

Nic stood to shake James's hand then signalled for another glass.

"You've only just arrived?" he asked as they both took a seat at the table in White's, avoiding James's question.

"Last night," James answered. "Abby and Alison called on Senna this morning to go shopping."

Nic's stomach flipped uncomfortably.

"And they told you about last night?"

"No. Robert came with them to tell me."

"He's worse than a Society biddy with his gossiping," Nic groused, earning himself a raised brow.

"I see he was right then," James said carefully.

A servant arrived with a clean tumbler and a second bottle of brandy. He must have sensed that Nic needed it.

"Right about what?" he asked, trying to remain as

calm as ever.

"About how you've changed. You're different. Something, or someone, is bothering you."

Nic didn't know what to say.

What could he say?

Your cousin is tying me in knots. I'm feeling things I haven't felt in years, maybe not ever. I'm terrified by how much I want her.

None of those seemed particularly appropriate things to say to a lady's overprotective cousin.

"Nothing is bothering me, James," he said, fighting to keep his tone even. "I don't trust Fulham and was surprised that Robert was encouraging the man's suit. But it is, of course, none of my business."

James frowned in response to the mention of Fulham.

"Robert didn't know anything about her invitation to Fulham until the bastard showed up," he said. "And he was about as happy about it as you apparently were."

"Yet he accompanied them, James, and you know as well as I do that Robert is the last person to be bothered by good manners or expectations." He paused. "Apart from Simon," he added, in the interest of honesty.

"Yes, and you know as well as I do that Robert is defenceless in the face of Abigail's wants. She agreed to let him join them. And Rob wasn't going to say no to that."

James rolled his eyes, and Nic had to laugh in spite of himself.

"Do you really think you're in a position to judge?" he asked dryly, laughing again at James's shamed face.

"That's beside the point." James grinned. "The good news is that Fulham will not be invited to join Alison at *any* event again. Won't get near her, if I have anything to do with it."

For a moment, James looked fierce and intimidating, not like his usual affable self.

It made Nic feel slightly better, even though he shouldn't be affected at all by what Alison Langton did or with whom she spent time.

"But here's the thing."

Nic's relief was short lived as James sat forward. His clear blue eyes, the exact colour of Alison's, bored into him.

"I know why I was unhappy to hear that Alison was throwing her lot in with Fulham. And I know why Robert was unhappy."

Nic refused to break eye contact. Refused to adjust his suddenly too-tight cravat.

"But I can't for the life of me figure out why it was bothering *you* so much."

Nic swallowed hard.

James wanted an explanation, which was all well and good. But Nic didn't have one, because Nic couldn't figure it out either.

"I suppose I've just gotten used to watching out for

you all over the years," he said finally.

James studied him carefully before nodding and sitting back in his chair.

"You have rather taken care of us all at one point or another over the years." He smiled. Nic thought he detected a hint of sadness or, God forbid, pity in the expression. "No wonder Simon has dubbed you Saint Nic."

Bloody Simon and his monikers. He was the only one who'd ever been proud of his.

"I'm no saint," Nic grumbled. And it was true.

He hadn't been saint-like in his youth, impregnating Ciara and then failing her.

And he felt as far from saint-like as was possible when he thought about Alison Langton and those eyes, that hair, that mouth…

"I really wouldn't know, since you don't exactly share much about your private life."

Another thing Nic really didn't want to discuss.

He wasn't sure why he withheld his work in St. Giles from his friends. He knew they would approve. Maybe even offer to help.

Perhaps it was because it was so personal to him. So much to do with Ciara and the baby. He didn't want to have to tell them about her. He would go to his grave never speaking a word of it to anyone.

It was just easier to keep people out of his life as much as he could.

Nobody could get hurt that way.

James sighed again.

"As you said, Nic, you've looked after us all. Not that I've given you much trouble. But – you need to look after yourself, too. And whilst I don't want to interfere, let me just say that if you were to grow to care for Alison – well, none of us would object."

Nic's heart thumped painfully at James's words.

Damn it all.

Had he been giving the impression that he cared for the girl?

That wouldn't do.

"James, I think there has been a misunderstanding. I –"

"No misunderstanding. Just me thinking out loud."

James stood and clapped Nic on the back.

"I believe we are all to attend Almack's tomorrow evening. Perhaps we'll see you there."

Nic didn't respond, merely watched James as he weaved his way through the tables on his way out the door.

If his friends were starting to think he was forming an attachment to Miss Langton, then he needed to stay away from her even more than he'd been doing.

In short, wherever she was, he needed not to be.

The Season couldn't last forever.

And he would just avoid her until she either married or went back home.

Chapter Twelve

NIC WAS ANGRIER with himself today than he'd been at the theatre.

Why was he standing in the bloody ballroom of Almack's Assembly Rooms?

Why hadn't he stayed away, like he was going to?

The major domo announced the arrival of the Duke and Duchess of Montvale, and Miss Alison Langton.

And there she was. The reason he hadn't stayed away.

Alison.

Nic swallowed the sudden lump in his throat.

She was ethereal. More beautiful than anyone he'd ever seen.

Her golden hair was piled in curls atop her head with loose tendrils brushing her bare shoulders, designed he was sure, to send him to Bedlam.

The gown was exquisite. The ice-blue silk making her eyes look like giant pools of the clearest water. Eyes a man could drown in, if he were foolish enough to fall into them.

He watched as a bevy of debutantes rushed forward to take Alison into their fold.

It appeared that it wasn't just the gentlemen of the *ton* who had fallen at her feet.

Speaking of said gentlemen, Nic watched them circling as soon as Alison had arrived. They were like damned bloodhounds, catching her scent the moment she walked through the door.

And it did nothing for his much-lauded equilibrium to see how they drooled over her.

He kept his distance as she was introduced to the patronesses.

These women could, he knew, make or ruin her. If they approved, she was sure to be considered an Incomparable. If they didn't, she could face social obscurity.

It was nonsense. But it was the world in which they lived.

The surge of protectiveness Nic felt as she walked toward them, her chin jutted out, her head high, was ridiculous.

He felt protective of the children he rescued in St. Giles, the women who saw and did things no human should have to.

That made sense.

This urge to rush over there and throw his weight behind Alison Langton did not.

Besides, she was the sister-in-law of the Duke of

Montvale and the cousin of the Marquess of Avondale. She didn't need him.

Still, his palms grew clammy, his nervousness acute as he watched the patronesses study Alison.

After a taut few moments, he saw them smile, and he was shocked at the pride and relief that coursed through him.

She looked so pleased that a tenderness he didn't want to feel wormed its way into his heart.

"Hello, Nic."

Nicholas turned at the sound of a voice behind him and smiled down at Senna Harrington, who looked stunning in emerald green.

"Senna, it's good to see you." Nic's smile was genuine as he kissed the young marchioness's cheek.

It was hard to believe that only three years ago, James and Senna hadn't even known each other.

Now, after tragedy brought them together and made them both wards of their niece Poppy, they were happily married and expecting a child of their own.

Nicholas had always liked Senna. And she had earned his unending respect and gratitude when she'd risked her own life to save James's.

"It looks like Alison has received the approval of the patronesses." Senna nodded her head toward where Alison stood, a red curl slipping over her brow with the action.

"Indeed," Nic answered, refusing to look over lest

he give himself away.

"And they're not the only ones who approve," Senna laughed. "Goodness. Her dance card will be filled before she opens it at this rate."

This time, Nic couldn't help himself, and he glared over in time to see Fulham, of all people, approach Alison, a predatory look on his face.

"Right, that's it," he said, and without even glancing back at Senna, he marched toward Alison and her many admirers.

"Miss Langton."

She turned at the sound of his voice, her blue eyes gazing up at him, and damned if he didn't feel the impact of them right in his very soul.

"Good evening, your grace."

Her curtsy was perfectly executed, but Nic couldn't help noticing the sparkle in her eyes had dimmed as soon as she'd looked at him.

And in spite of himself, he missed it.

"Would you do me the honour of dancing the next with me, Miss Langton?"

Her eyes widened and for a moment, he thought he saw joy in their blue depths.

But she blinked, and it was gone.

"I'm afraid Miss Langton has already agreed to dance the next with me, your grace."

The nasally voice of Lord Fulham grated on Nicholas's nerves, and he turned a cold stare on the man.

Nicholas knew he was going to see his smug face again tonight or more likely, tomorrow morning when he'd staggered out of one of his usual haunts. The less than salubrious haunts that Nic kept an eye on.

Nic didn't have a problem with vices.

Lord knew, he wouldn't have been friends with Simon, of all people, if he had.

But Simon only ever gamed at reputable hells. And never treated women of any class poorly.

The same could not be said of the blackguard standing before him now.

The orchestra plucked the opening strands of the waltz, something Alison should absolutely not be dancing with Fulham, and Nic could do nothing but watch as Fulham smirked insolently at him before taking hold of her arm and leading her to join the other dancers.

Nicholas glared around the room.

Where were her guardians? The ones who weren't going to let Fulham near her?

Robert was nowhere to be seen, and James had been unsurprisingly accosted by a group of matriarchs.

The *ton* loved James. And at any given time, he could be found surrounded by more than one admirer.

Stay out of it, Nicholas told himself. *She's none of your business.*

He looked back in the direction of the dancers, and his jaw clenched as he watched Fulham lean over to whisper in Alison's ear.

Didn't the bastard have a care for her reputation? For what people would say seeing him paw at her in public? She had only just received the approval of Almack's patronesses.

He knew he should leave well enough alone.

But reason had deserted him.

He strode across the room, oblivious to everyone and everything but her.

Fulham turned Alison to face him, his hand resting too low on her waist, her body pulled too close to his.

Before they could move, Nic stepped forward and tapped the other man none-too-gently on the shoulder.

He took a perverse sort of pleasure in Fulham's scowl of displeasure.

"What are you about, Barnbury?" the other man snapped.

Nicholas gave him his haughtiest ducal glare and revelled in Fulham's gulp.

"The lady is dancing this set with me," he said quietly, firmly.

There was a tense silence between the two gentlemen as Fulham obviously considered what to do.

Finally, Nic saw defeat in the smaller man's eyes and with a grimace of displeasure, Fulham turned and stomped away.

Feeling rather smug, Nic turned to face Alison, a rare, genuine smile lighting his face.

That smile quickly disappeared however in the face of her palpable anger. She was glaring at him, her eyes narrowed, her lips pursed.

She looked like an angry little kitten, harmless and endearing, though Nic instinctively knew not to say as much.

The strains of the waltz echoed around the room, and Nic took Alison in his arms, finding it harder than ever to ignore the feeling of *rightness* of having her there.

She was still glaring at him, still angry. But even knowing that she was furious with him couldn't dampen the scorching desire that inflamed his very blood just from holding her like this.

"What exactly do you think you're doing, your grace?" she bit out, holding herself stiffly, head still tilted toward his so she could ontinue glaring at him.

She was close enough that he could smell the floral scent of her, see the silver flecks in her eyes.

"I'm dancing, Miss Langton," he answered evenly, rather enjoying himself now that she was away from Fulham and in his arms.

Her eyes narrowed at his flippant response.

"Yes, but I didn't agree to dance this set with you. I agreed to dance it with Lord Fulham."

"But he's not here," he answered smoothly, allowing himself a small smile. "I am."

"Because you ran him off," she bit out angrily.

"You know, I'm starting to get mightily offended, Miss Langton. One would think you didn't wish to dance with me."

Her mouth popped open, and it took all of his strength not to dip his head and capture it with his own.

That night on Simon's balcony when she'd pressed her lips against his own still haunted him.

It hadn't been a kiss. Not a real one. He'd been so shocked by her actions, and his reaction to it, that he hadn't even responded. Merely pushed her away and refused to let himself think on it again.

But if he kissed her now–

"I rather thought it would be the other way around," she said eventually, interrupting his thoughts. "You don't exactly give the impression that you crave my company, your grace."

Nic sobered at the hurt in her tone.

Though her comment had been, he was sure, intended as light-hearted, there was no denying the truth in it.

It was unfair of him, he knew. To blow hot and cold on her. To ignore and disparage her one moment, then act like a jealous beau the next.

The truth was that he *did* crave her company. But he shouldn't.

Still, his turmoil was not her fault.

Had he not felt this intense, heated, overwhelming

attraction to her the second he'd met her, he would have been more courteous, Nic knew.

Wasn't courtesy what he was famed for, after all? As the cousin of one close friend, and the sister-in-law of another, he would have paid more attention to Alison. Danced with her more. Been nicer. Actually had more than a ten-second conversation with her.

An uncomfortable guilt gnawed at him. And not the guilt that lived within his soul every day. But a new one. One borne of his bad behaviour and not the tragic circumstances of his past.

He looked down into the beautiful face of the woman in his arms and realised she was awaiting an answer.

He could try to say something charming, flirtatious even, like Simon would. Or give her a disarming smile, like James.

Robert would probably just say something insulting.

But Nic was nothing if not honest to a fault. And he wasn't devilish like Simon, or charming like James, or brutal like Robert.

"I have craved your company, Miss Langton," he said softly, sincerely. "I haven't wanted to. But believe me, I have."

Her eyes widened, and he heard her breath hitch.

"Oh," she finally whispered which, given her penchant for saying things that drove him mad, was a first.

There was a moment of deafening silence before she frowned slightly and spoke again.

"I don't know why you shouldn't crave my company, you know," she said, sounding much more like her maddening self. "I don't wish to sound arrogant, your grace. But I've never really met anyone who wished he didn't want to be around me."

"I can well believe it," Nic said matter-of-factly.

No man in his right mind would avoid her on purpose.

He hadn't been in his right mind in years.

"Then, why –"

"Miss Langton," he interrupted, not wanting to even try to explain the confusion of his thoughts about her. "I apologise. I should have been – kinder. Would you do me the honour of taking a drive with me tomorrow afternoon?"

Once again, her mouth popped open in surprise.

Once again, Nic had to steel himself not to take advantage.

He was tired of worrying about the girl from a distance. If Robert and James weren't going to keep her away from Fulham and his ilk, then Nic would. If that meant spending his days with her instead of avoiding her at all costs, then that's what he would do.

"You mean you want to voluntarily spend time with me?" she asked dryly.

She was a minx, of that there was no doubt.

And damned if he didn't find it almost painfully attractive.

"If you will permit it, yes."

She eyed him suspiciously, the dancers around them forgotten by them both.

"Is this just to keep me away from Lord Fulham?" she asked, far too astutely for his liking.

Again, his sense of honesty reared its head.

"In part, yes," he answered truthfully, his heart hammering at the disappointment that flitted across her face.

She was quiet for an age.

The dance came to a halt, and Nic found himself having to work at letting her go.

"I'll come on one condition," she finally said as he escorted her back to the edge of the ballroom.

His lips quirked.

"And what's that?"

"I want to go to Gunther's," she said suddenly, the light of challenge sparking in her eyes. "Everyone goes on and on about how delicious the ices are. I want one. And I want you to have one. It's frivolous and silly and unimportant. And I want to go."

Nic was sure Alison thought he would refuse to waste his afternoon doing something so frivolous.

And truth be told, he rarely spent his afternoons away from St. Giles and the orphanages and home he patronised.

But he was suddenly loathe to have Alison think he was – what had she called him? *A boring old fuddy-duddy.*

So, just this once, he would allow himself to shirk responsibilities and prove that he could have fun.

"You have yourself a deal, Miss Langton."

Chapter Thirteen

"OH, ALLY YOU look wonderful."

Alison brushed her hands nervously down her skirts for the hundredth time. At least it kept her from wringing them.

She was a ball of nervous excitement.

Last night, Lord Barnbury had been – well, wonderful.

Much as it had angered her that he had swooped in and taken over the waltz, she could admit to herself that inside she'd been ecstatic.

He hadn't danced another with her, and Lord Fulham had been all cordiality when he'd come to claim a reel, since he'd been robbed of the waltz.

However, James had stepped in, declaring it time for them to leave.

Alison should have been irritated by her cousin's high-handedness. But after her dance with Nicholas, after the change in him, the glimpse of the fun, charismatic man lurking beneath the sombre surface, nothing could have dampened her mood.

She'd floated home on a cloud of expectation.

Now she was in the drawing room, awaiting Nicholas's arrival and hoping desperately that he hadn't reverted to the grump he usually was around her.

"Do you think so?" she asked now, biting her lip.

"Of course," Abby answered immediately. "You'd look wonderful in a sack, my dear. But lemon is so becoming on you."

It had taken Alison an age to pick what to wear for her afternoon with Lord Barnbury. She must have tried on fifty gowns before poor Eliza could escape to fetch her a white spencer, and white bonnet trimmed with a lemon ribbon to match the colour of her walking dress.

As she'd expected, Robert and Abigail had been thrilled to hear of the plan. And whilst none of them, especially not Alison, would mistake it as an attempt at courtship, it was nice to see Lord Barnbury trying to be kind.

In the secret parts of her heart, parts she refused to give any credence to, Alison wondered if the duke might be coming to like her just a little.

His words last night had been so cryptic. He had said that he craved her company, but that he shouldn't.

Those words both confused and excited her in equal measure.

A gurgle from her niece shook Alison from her reverie, and she looked over to see Lottie beaming up at her, her huge blue eyes studying her intently.

Alison's heart melted.

She had never considered herself the maternal sort. Yet looking at Charlotte now, so lovely in her mama's arms, she felt a pang of longing.

Alison reached over and plucked the babe from Abigail's arms, delighted in Lottie's squeal.

She cradled the baby against her, inhaling the scent of her soft, downy curls.

"She'll drool on your gown," Abigail laughingly warned her.

A knock on the door sounded, and Alison's heart leapt from her chest.

He was here!

She caught Abigail's knowing smirk and felt her cheeks heat.

Before she could scold her sister, however, the door swung open, and there he was.

Alison's breath caught, not at the duke's handsomeness, which still admittedly took her breath away, but at the look in his eyes as he stared at Alison and Lottie.

It was so intense that she felt it to the depths of her soul.

At first, the navy depths lit with a fiery desire so strong that Alison felt as though it could scorch her skin.

But in the next moment, they turned so bleak, so desolate that it pained her to look into them.

What on earth could have caused such a look of

abject misery to haunt his eyes?

Alison wanted to reach out to him, to offer comfort for a pain she didn't even understand.

But within the blink of an eye, all trace of emotion was gone. And he had reverted to the cool, calm, unflappable duke he ever was.

Alison was coming to learn that he could mask any real emotion more easily than anyone she'd ever met before.

"Good afternoon, Abigail. Good afternoon, Miss Langton."

He bowed to the two ladies, seeming completely at ease.

But Alison knew she hadn't imagined that look, and it just made him all the more intriguing to her.

"If you're ready, Miss Langton, my phaeton is outside."

"Of course." She smiled, feeling inexplicably shy.

Last night when she'd teased him about taking her for ices and being frivolous, she had felt confident in his company.

Now, she felt unsure of herself.

Abby rushed forward to take Lottie from Alison's arms.

"Goodbye, sweetling." Alison bent to kiss Lottie's cheek.

She straightened up and watched as Lord Barnbury reached out a finger and gently stroked the baby's cheek. Her stomach fluttered alarmingly as a potent desire unfurled inside her at the small action.

Gracious! How wanton of her.

"I'm ready, your grace," she mumbled, feeling the heat in her cheeks.

She swept out the door before him, studiously ignoring her sister's smirk as she went.

NIC TOOK THE time that he helped Alison into the high-seated conveyance to gather himself.

Seeing Bonnie the other day and being reminded of Alison had shaken him.

Seeing Lottie in the arms of her aunt had floored him.

Nic had often wondered what it was about Alison Langton that got under his skin so much, from the first second he'd seen her.

Watching her hold the niece that looked so like her had been a blinding revelation.

Though they were nothing alike, in either looks or mannerisms, Alison's build was similar to that of Ciara's; her height, her figure. Her blonde hair, though always perfectly coiffed unlike a maid's would ever be, was a similar colour. And they both had a *joie de vivre* that was infectious. Though Nic had avoided Alison's natural light and warmth thus far.

Seeing Alison hold Lottie had brought to mind an imagine of Ciara holding their babe. And that made him realise that the first, immediate effect Alison had on him had been because for a split second, she'd reminded him of the woman he'd failed in the most unforgiveable way.

Everything after that first moment however, he thought wryly, had been all Alison. And now that he knew her better, how she ever could have reminded him of Ciara was beyond him.

Upon seeing Alison hold Lottie, the desire and something else that coursed through him, had been overwhelming. But in that same moment, he remembered Ciara and the baby he'd lost, and his heart had twisted with sorrow. How could a single woman cause him to experience both fascination and pain?

How could he ever contemplate being a father when he'd had the chance and let down both Ciara and his child in the most heinous of ways?

Hastily gathering his control he made certain Alison was secure, and he circled the phaeton to his seat.

Only last night he had promised himself that he would just be in Miss Langton's company, keep his head, and retain his lauded equipoise.

He climbed into the vehicle, turning to face Alison.

She was beaming at him. Bedecked in lemon and white, her hair shining in the summer sun, her blue eyes sparkling like pools of warm, exotic waters, she looked like a breath of fresh air. A young, carefree innocent who didn't need to be dragged into his complicated and unhappy past.

The problem was that Nic was finding it increasingly difficult to keep her out.

He found himself wanting to share the truth with her, wanting to explain why he kept her at such a distance. And why he found it so hard to.

"So, I believe you demanded ices, Miss Langton?"

Her laughter was like a balm to her soul.

"I requested ices, your grace. Very politely."

His own laugh joined hers.

"Very politely." He grinned, feeling younger and lighter than he had in years.

He eased the pair of greys into the busy flow of traffic and riders, silent as he navigated the bustling street.

"Thank you, your grace."

He looked over at the timid statement, surprised to see her eyes lowered in an uncharacteristically demure fashion.

"What for, Miss Langton?"

She glanced up at him then, her cheeks flushed pink, making him ache to touch her.

"For deciding to forgive me for whatever crime I had committed when we first met. And for – well, for accosting you on Simon's balcony," she blurted.

Nic felt that new, uncomfortable guilt fill him

again.

He'd been unfair. He knew that.

Miss Langton was spoilt and frivolous, perhaps a little shallow.

There was nothing wrong with that. She was a beautiful young lady experiencing her first Season. She should be frivolous and shallow.

It wasn't her fault that Nic was so fiercely attracted to her. Nor was it her fault that he could never be with someone like her.

Nicholas's past had changed him in a fundamental way. He could do nothing other than dedicate his life to helping others, to trying to somehow assuage the guilt that was so much a part of him now.

It was just who he was.

And someone like him didn't belong with someone like her.

But for now, for today, he could simply try to enjoy being in her company. Even knowing that the gap between them was too wide and always would be.

"You committed no crime," he said softly. "I was – frustrated. By things that were out of your control… and apparently mine."

He could see her confusion at his cryptic remark, but he wasn't about to confess the almost unbearable attraction he felt toward her. And he sure as hell wasn't going anywhere near a conversation about kissing her.

"Now, tell me what flavour you demanded – er,

requested," he laughed.

Her frown cleared, and that smile lit her face once more.

"I have no idea," she said excitedly. "There are many, are there not? I want to try them all."

"Well then." He nodded. "All it is."

Chapter Fourteen

S HE WAS THOROUGHLY enjoying herself, Alison decided some time later. Perilously so. Her heart was in more danger than ever today, when Nicholas was being so charming. So light-hearted!

They'd talked and laughed and joked about the *beau monde* and the stark differences between English and American Society.

He had a wicked sense of humour, and his commentary on the *ton* and its members was both riveting and hilarious.

Now, he'd gone across the road to Gunther's to procure her much anticipated ices.

She'd laughingly objected when he'd declared that he would get one of every flavour.

Of course, he wouldn't. He couldn't!

Alison looked around, soaking up the comings and goings around her. As with everywhere else Abigail had described to her, Gunther's was positively brimming with Quality, and Alison was pleased with the number of greetings being called her way.

She seemed to have well and truly secured herself

as a success in Town.

Only weeks ago, that would have thrilled Alison, for it would have meant that she would have her pick of beaux.

Now, though she was relieved and pleased, the idea of a husband was anathema to her.

The truth was that she hadn't met a single gentleman she was interested in.

Except one.

As though her thoughts had conjured him, Nicholas appeared, and Alison clasped a hand over her mouth.

He was carrying a silver tray filled with glass bowls of ices in different colours.

And behind him were two servants, carrying identical trays filled with even more bowls.

She laughed aloud as he sauntered toward her, uncaring about the gasps, whispers, and stares all around him.

"My dear Miss Langton." He bowed elaborately as he reached the phaeton. "Your selection."

He handed her the tray before jumping lightly into the driver's seat.

Then he reached over and took the trays from the waiting servants, one in each hand.

"Where are we going to put all of this?" Alison gasped.

"Hmm. I don't suppose you want to eat all of

them?"

"I don't think I *could* eat all of them," she laughed. "I can't believe you got all of them."

"You wanted all of them," he answered simply, but Alison's heart flew as though he'd declared his love for her. "Why don't you try them and pick what you like?"

She bit her lip, running her eyes over the melting ices, trying to decide which one looked the best. "Don't you want a taste?"

She looked up when he didn't answer to find him watching her, his eyes gleaming with a heat that seared her skin.

She felt trapped in that gaze, unable to look away, unable to breathe.

A sudden shout from across the street rent the air, and Nicholas's eyes snapped away from hers.

Alison heaved a breath, her heart thundering.

She wasn't quite sure what had just happened, but it felt as though something had shifted between them.

Feeling feverish, she reached for a lemon ice and began to eat it with the delicate silver spoon.

She was quite sure it was delicious. But she couldn't taste a thing.

NICHOLAS'S HEART WAS thundering so loudly, he was surprised Alison couldn't hear it.

Get a hold of yourself, man he told himself over and over.

Being this close to her, smelling that floral scent, watching the summer breeze play with loose tendrils of her hair was torture enough.

His lust had been thrumming through his veins from the second he'd laid eyes on her.

Seeing her delight when he'd arrived with one ice and sorbet of every flavour on the menu had awakened something infinitely more potent and dangerous than desire. Tenderness.

He'd raised more than one eyebrow during his purchase, and he knew the *ton* well enough to know that tongues would be wagging.

But Nic didn't care. It had all been worth it to see her face light up with joy.

But then she'd asked him if he wanted a taste and God help him, he'd nearly ravished her there and then. In full view of the *ton*.

It had taken Herculean effort just to look away from her.

This situation was fast getting outside his control. And that wasn't something he was used to. In fact, he always made sure every single part of his life was rigidly under his control.

But that was before Alison Langton.

However, he couldn't sit here in turmoil. And he wouldn't punish Alison again for his own shortcomings by regressing to a surly, unpleasant boor.

He turned back to face her, bracing for the impact of her.

"The lemon," he smiled. "A good choice."

She stared at him for a moment before blinking rapidly.

"Oh, y-yes. It matched my gown," she said wryly.

She heaved a breath then looked around her.

"I'm afraid these will go to waste, your grace."

"Nonsense," he answered immediately. "You wanted to try them all, and I would have been remiss had I not made sure that your first Gunther's experience was everything you could possibly want."

She beamed at him, and he had to swallow past a sudden lump in his throat.

"Do you think we could drop the formal title?" he suddenly blurted. "I hate it at the best of times."

"But that wouldn't be at all proper, your grace," she said then her mouthed lifted in an expression that was pure devilment. "And we know you are such a champion of propriety."

He couldn't help the answering quirk of his own lips.

"You are a hoyden, Miss Langton," he scolded with faux seriousness. "But I think buying up the whole tearoom should at least get me a Christian name."

She giggled, shaking her head.

"Very well," she conceded. "I shall call you Nicholas. And you shall call me Alison."

The idea pleased Nic more than it should and not trusting himself to speak, he merely nodded.

They spent an enjoyable ten minutes laughingly tasting the rapidly melting ices.

Eventually, however, they had to admit defeat, and Nic signalled for the servants to come and collect the trays and glasses.

"I feel ashamed to have wasted so much of it," Alison said. "But I couldn't eat another bite."

"Did we at least succeed in finding your favourite?" he asked.

She bit her lip in concentration while she considered the options, and it was all Nic could do not to groan aloud at the action.

Finally, she shrugged.

"I cannot pick one," she said. "There were far too many delicious choices."

"Well then, we'll just try again next time," he said.

Her eyes snapped up to his, and he could see clearly the delight swimming in their depths.

"Next time?" she asked.

Nic's heart hammered in his chest.

He smiled softly down at her.

"Next time," he said.

As they drove home, Alison chattered beside him the entire way.

Her *joie de vivre* was infectious, and Nic found

himself laughing out loud at her outrageous statements and opinions on life as an American in England.

He forgot about being self-contained. Forgot about always been sombre and serious. He just talked and laughed and enjoyed the company of the woman he hadn't been able to stop thinking about for a year.

When they reached Robert's townhouse, only steps from his own, Nic was surprised at how disappointed he was to be saying goodbye to her.

He jumped from the phaeton, tossing the reins to a waiting footman, then hurried around to lift her down.

She weighed nothing at all and as his hands spanned her waist and he lifted her, placing her slowly on her feet, the flame of his desire crackled to life.

He wanted more than anything to bend his head and capture her mouth in a kiss that he was sure would change him for life.

It was only sheer force of will keeping him from doing so.

And that force of will was weakening by the second.

"Alison, I –"

"Ah, there you are."

Nic swore softly under his breath as Rob appeared in the doorway of his house.

Though his friend looked calm enough, Nic didn't miss that he was watching them quite shrewdly.

He stepped away from Alison, cursing his friend's

interruption.

It might have been wishful thinking, but he could have sworn he saw regret in Alison's eyes, too.

Might it be possible that she had wanted his kiss?

She turned away from him and darted up the steps and into the house, leaving him to trail behind her.

Once he reached eye level with Robert, Nic found he couldn't hold his friend's speculative stare, and he stepped inside the house without invitation, never having needed one.

He followed a glimpse of lemon toward the drawing room, his feet pulling him after her, even before his mind caught up.

This, he knew, was not good.

Dropping his guard for one afternoon had made him even more susceptible to her.

Feelings that he'd been able to bury were becoming harder to ignore. Terrifying, impossible feelings.

"Drink?"

He jumped at the sound of Robert's voice just behind him.

"What are you doing, sneaking up on me?" he snapped.

"I didn't sneak up on you," Robert answered. There was a slight pause. "Perhaps you were just distracted."

The astute look in Robert's grey eyes made Nic nervous, and he cleared his throat.

"And you must stay and dine with us, Nic," this

from Abby, who was sitting beside Alison on a chaise by the window.

The sisters were incredibly alike with matching bright blonde hair and big, blue eyes.

Why then could he look at Abigail, see how beautiful she was, and feel nothing?

Why did he look at Alison and feel like she was a part of him he hadn't even known was missing?

A panic began to claw at him, slithering along his veins and making his heart beat faster.

He'd never considered himself a coward, but these feelings were scaring him. He needed to get away from here. Away from her.

"Oh, yes." Alison smiled up at him, her blue eyes so trusting, "Please, do."

Nic's heart was thundering, terrified at the changes this slip of a girl had wrought in him.

He'd abandoned his responsibilities to take her out for the afternoon. Now, after swearing to himself that he'd never love again he was –

Nic shied away from a feeling he wasn't ready to face.

"I can't," he blurted.

Robert, Abigail, and Alison frowned in confusion at his outburst.

"I-I have somewhere to be. If you'll excuse me?"

With the briefest of bows, and avoiding eye contact with Alison, he turned and rushed from the room as though the hounds of Hell were chasing him, putting as much distance as possible between himself and everything he was feeling in that room.

Chapter Fifteen

"GRACIOUS, ALLY. WHAT did you do to him?"

Alison shrugged helplessly, trying to mask the hurt and disappointment she was feeling.

It was foolish, of course, to be *hurt* because the man wasn't staying to dinner.

But – well, she couldn't shake the feeling that he had been running away just now.

Where could he need to be at this hour? It was too late to call on anyone, and Abby had said that Nicholas tended to attend the same events as they.

There was nothing to rush away for that evening.

The only thing happening worth any notice was a musical evening at Lady Amberley's, something Robert refused to attend on the grounds that he wasn't sure he'd wake from the sleep the event would induce. And if Robert wasn't going to attend, then the chances were Nicholas wasn't going to, either.

Alison had had no objections to attending the evening with her sister earlier.

Whilst she'd been awaiting Nicholas's arrival, she wouldn't have objected to anything.

Now – well now that he'd run off, an uneventful evening filled with nothing but music and time to obsess about the confounding duke didn't sound all that appealing.

She remembered what Lord Fulham had said the other day, about Nic being an avid gambler who frequented the hells around St. Giles.

It just didn't seem true to her. He was always so conscientious, so proper. Would he really be the type of man who haphazardly gambled all the time?

It wasn't that she objected, per se. It just seemed out of character.

The other alternative was that he was frequenting *another* type of establishment in The Rookery. Something she probably shouldn't know about, being a young, unmarried lady.

But she wasn't naïve, and she wasn't stupid.

She should have asked him about it. It would bother her until she knew the truth. Niggle at her like an itch she couldn't scratch. But she was too afraid of hearing something she didn't want to know. Too afraid that the truth would hurt her somehow.

Alison jumped to her feet, angry at herself for overthinking everything so much. This was exactly why she needed to go out this evening. To be distracted from any and all thoughts of Nicholas Fyfe.

"Shall we get ready to go, Abigail? I'm quite looking forward to Lady Amberley's musicale."

She rushed from the room, lest her sister ask her any more questions about the Duke of Barnbury.

The last thing she wanted was to talk about him.

"It's just surprising, that's all. He seems so different lately. And we don't see him half as much as we used to."

Alison gritted her teeth as Abigail continued to prattle on about Nicholas.

Ordinarily, she would be more than happy to discuss the duke in minor detail. But not tonight, when she needed a break from her thoughts and feelings about the exasperating man.

"Good evening, your grace. Miss Langton."

Alison was relieved by the interruption and looked up to see Miss Harriet Billings smiling down at them.

She had met Miss Billings at a few previous Society events. She was a pleasant, quiet girl. Not exactly riveting but nice enough and more importantly, a distraction from Abigail's monologue about Nicholas.

"Good evening, Miss Billings. How well you look tonight. Please, join us." Abby indicated an empty chair beside Alison.

Miss Billings took a seat, her ruffled skirts fanning out around her.

"Are you enjoying the performances?" Alison

asked.

"Oh, yes." Miss Billings smiled. "I confess myself rather nervous that I will be called upon. Mama likes me to play for people, but I get so anxious."

Alison's heart went out to the young girl. Mrs. Billings certainly seemed to push her daughter into the centre of attention at any given opportunity. And Harriet Billings didn't seem the type to enjoy that sort of thing.

"I'm sure you will do wonderfully well." Alison smiled.

"Do you play or sing, Miss Langton?"

She did, as it happened. And did both reasonably well. But she was of no mind to do so that evening.

"I'm afraid not," Alison said evenly, ignoring Abby's raised brow. "But I look forward to hearing everyone else."

The ladies chatted for a while longer before Mrs. Billings marched over, demanding her daughter perform.

Alison grimaced in support.

Miss Billings, as it turned out, was a lovely singer and pianoforte player.

Alison watched her, feeling desperately sorry for the girl whose cheeks were scarlet the entire time she performed.

Afterwards, she was about to make her way over when she noticed Lord Fulham head in Harriet's direction.

If possible, the girl's cheeks coloured further still.

She looked well and truly dazzled by the blonde-haired lord.

Lord Fulham had, until this evening, paid particularly close attention to Alison. Yet tonight, he had yet to speak to her.

Alison wondered at herself for not caring a jot.

She had no interest in Lord Fulham, or anyone else.

As she watched, however, Lord Fulham's gaze moved to hers as though watching for her reaction.

Did he expect she'd be jealous? Should she be jealous?

She huffed out a breath of consternation.

As she had feared, Nicholas Fyfe had completely ruined her for anyone else.

IT HAD BEEN three days.

Three excruciating days.

And though Nic had spent most of his time in St. Giles, throwing himself into his causes like never before, he had noticed every day. Every hour. Every second.

Because they were days, hours, and seconds he spent away from Alison.

It didn't help that every morning when he opened

the papers, he read something about his afternoon with her. Though he prided himself on not reading the scandal sheets, he hadn't been able to resist a peek.

Has London's newest diamond achieved what none of us thought possible, and caught the attention of the bachelor duke?

Has the mysterious Duke of B succumbed to cupid's bow in the form of the blonde-haired, blue-eed American beauty who has taken Town by storm?

It appears that with all of London falling at her feet, nobody is immune to the charms of Miss L. Why even our esteemed Lord B seems to have fallen for the lady's favours.

What the hell had happened to him?

How had he gone from finding her spoilt and irritating to feeling like he couldn't breathe without her around?

They hadn't even kissed, for God's sake. Well, unless you counted the time she acosted him on Simon's balcony over a year ago.

Over the last couple of days, he had tried to convince himself that he was perhaps just starved of female company.

But the idea of being with another woman didn't appeal in the slightest. If anything, it made him feel bizarrely guilty for even considering it.

So, he'd just skulked around the homes and hospitals he funded, feeling miserable and confused.

The problem was that he'd come to actually *like* Alison Langton, beyond being more viscerally attracted to her than anyone before.

Yes, she was playful and a little spoilt. But she was bright, and bubbly, and light-hearted. She loved her family; she was kind to everyone he saw her with. And spending time with her made him smile more than he had in years.

But the fact remained, they were and always would be unsuited.

The events of Nic's life, the tragedy of Ciara's loss, and the loss of his child had made Nic a completely different person. A person who wasn't particularly interested in the glittering world to which he belonged. A person who had spent the last ten years of his life dedicated to helping those less fortunate, feeling guilty for the wealth and privilege to which he'd been born, and doing his best to share it around.

Alison Langton had come here to find a husband who was at the centre of that world. She wanted parties and frivolity. A social life befitting a member of the Peerage.

He couldn't imagine her wanting to spend her days helping children from the streets, or prostitutes who found themselves in trouble.

And he would never ask it of her.

Nic barely had the stomach for some of the things he encountered on the streets of St. Giles. He would never wish to expose Alison to the things he witnessed. The depravity he was surrounded by every day of his life.

And so, that left a gap between them that would never be closed. They were worlds apart from each other, in more ways than one.

Nic didn't know if he'd ever marry. Though he knew he had a duty to his title, he was happy to allow a cousin to inherit it all.

If he left this world alone, on the periphery of his friends' lives, then that would be enough for him. At least he knew that by keeping everyone at a distance, he couldn't hurt them.

He convinced himself of this.

And then he imagined Alison at all the events she was sure to be attending. Bedecked in her finery and looking like an angel. The gentlemen of the *ton* falling at her feet.

He imagined her choosing one of her many admirers. Marrying. Filling a nursery. Belonging to someone else.

And the jealousy that tore through him was excruciating.

Finally, now, after three days, he admitted defeat.

He wanted to see her.

Foolish though it was.

He left his house, feeling lighter than he had in days at the mere prospect of being in her company, and walked the short distance to Robert's.

Though it was past the dinner hour, and nowhere near usual visiting times, Robert, James, Simon, and Nic had always treated each other's homes like their own.

Nobody would bat an eyelid at Nic turning up now.

In fact, when the footman opened the door, nobody even suggested announcing him, given the late hour. There would be no member of the *ton* there to comment on the lack of ceremony, and so he strode toward the drawing room where he knew the family would be.

Reaching the room, Nic opened the door and walked in.

Robert and Abigail sprang apart, and judging from the flush on Abby's cheeks, they had been doing something Nic would rather not think about.

"I hope I'm not interrupting," Nic said wryly, his eyes scanning the room.

Surely they wouldn't have been acting that way in front of Alison?

The rest of the room was empty.

She wasn't here.

"You are, as a matter of fact," Robert said, pulling Abigail under his arm when she tried to move away.

Nic ignored the altogether ridiculous envy that coursed through him at Rob's freedom to act however he wanted with the woman he lov – well, never mind. His mind hastily skittered from that particular train of thought.

He grinned at Rob's grumpiness.

At least Rob had the decency to stop. If he'd walked in on Simon and Amelia, he was sure he'd have gotten quite the show.

Nic desperately wanted to ask about Alison, but he didn't want to be too obvious, lest he raise questions he wasn't willing or able to answer.

"You are not out tonight?"

Rob raised a brow. "Well," he said with a smirk. "We're here. So, no."

There was a tense silence as husband and wife merely gazed at him.

"Y-you are alone? That is – you don't have company?"

Abigail frowned up at Rob in confusion. Nic didn't blame her. It wasn't as though he were making any sense.

"Um, no," she responded politely. "Lottie is abed. It is just us."

She must bloody well know he wasn't enquiring about Lottie.

Nic tried not to let any frustration show.

There was another tense pause before Rob chuckled softy and moved to his drinks table.

"If you want to know where Ally is, Nic, just ask."

Nic froze at Robert's softly spoken words.

He glanced at Abby, who was smiling at him, back to Rob, who had by now filled a tumbler of brandy and was holding it out to him.

Nic tried not to let his hand shake as he accepted the glass.

What was he to say to that?

He wasn't used to feeling wrong-footed. And he certainly wasn't used to being the one teased in their friendship circle.

"I-I don't know what you mean," he managed to croak before downing the contents of his glass.

Once more, silence descended, and Nic cursed the pair of them to Perdition.

Finally, he couldn't take it anymore.

"Now that you mention it." He tried and probably failed to sound casual. "Where is Miss Langton this evening?"

He scowled at Rob's snort.

Abigail at least took pity on him, for she shot daggers at Rob before turning back to Nic.

"She is at Vauxhall Gardens tonight," she said casually. "Miss Harriet Billings invited her along."

Nic frowned, not at all happy with this turn of events.

He knew the Gardens would appeal to Alison. The

fireworks, the fountains, the follies and secret pathways. She would love such a place.

But along with the whimsical, there was a real potential for a young lady to find herself in trouble.

Of everywhere in London that the *beau monde* frequented, Vauxhall Gardens was the least decorous, the least inhibited.

Classes mixed, merchants and servants rubbing shoulders with Peers. And more than one person had been known to throw caution to the wind there.

Nic couldn't believe that Rob would let Ally go there alone.

"I'm not familiar with Miss Billings," he said, trying not to panic. "Is her family well known?"

"Her father and I have met briefly," Rob said. "They seem decent enough."

"And her father is going, too, is he?" Nic bit out.

Rob and Abby shared a brief glance, which annoyed him further still.

"No, Miss Billings mentioned that her brother would be escorting them. He is an officer of His Majesty's army," she said reassuringly.

A soldier.

That was bloody worse! Nic had met far too many soldiers around the streets of St. Giles to entrust Alison's safety to one.

"And you just let her go off, did you?" He rounded on Robert, sense and reason gone. "With a group of soldiers and a girl whose family you barely know? What the hell were you thinking?"

Rob narrowed his eyes at Nic's furious criticism.

"If I thought she would be in danger, Nic, I wouldn't have let her go."

"And how do you *know* whether she's in danger or not?" he snarled. "It seems you've been more than a little preoccupied."

Abigail's face fell at Nic's words, and he felt a twist of guilt in his gut, which he ignored.

Rationally, he knew both Abby and Rob were dedicated to giving Alison a successful and safe Season. That they would never purposely endanger her.

But rationality had no place in his mind right now.

"Nic –"

He heard the warning in Rob's tone, but he was past caring.

"Robert, do you think we should have let her go?" Abigail sounded distressed but once more, Nic refused to feel guilty for it.

"I'm going to go and see that she is well," he snapped.

Robert sighed. "I'll come with you," he said. "And you need to calm down."

"I'm not waiting," Nic spoke over his friend.

In some part of his mind, he knew he was laying himself bare. Opening himself up to interrogation, but without awaiting an answer from either of them, he turned on his heel and marched from the room.

He wanted to find Alison and make sure she was safe.

After that he could worry about the consequences of how revealing his actions were.

Chapter Sixteen

A LISON WAS ENTHRALLED by the sights and sounds around her.

When Miss Billings had sent a note inviting her to join their party to Vauxhall Gardens, Alison had been thrilled. Not least because it would be a good distraction from three miserable days wondering why Nicholas had disappeared once again.

At first, Abby had objected to her accepting the invitation. And Robert had outright refused.

But through cajoling, pleading, begging, and dangling the prospect of an evening alone together in front of them, they'd finally conceded.

Robert had interrogated Captain Billings, Harriet's brother, when their carriage had arrived to take Alison to Vauxhall and had satisfied himself that she was in good hands.

The Captain and his friend had been attentive to Harriet and Alison all evening, securing them a box and making sure they weren't approached by any of the more questionable gentlemen who walked by.

This place was like nothing she'd ever seen.

There were acrobatic performers, a gazebo for dancing, and a maze of walkways lit with lanterns and dotted with fountains and hidden loveseats.

There were even faux ruins in the middle, to her amazement.

It was exciting. Magical, even.

And though she wished she were experiencing it with Nicholas, she was determined to enjoy every moment of it.

She had already danced with Captain Billings, an unassuming and quiet gentleman much like his sister, and his friend Captain Sorrell, who waxed lyrical about the girl he planned to marry once he returned home to his native Scotland.

Alison found herself overcome with envy as Captain Sorrell spoke excitedly of his plans to wed.

She couldn't imagine anything more wonderful than a quiet life in the countryside with the person she loved.

The glamour and excitement of London was all very well, but she could well imagine that it could lose its shine rather quickly.

It was exhilarating, but vacuous. There didn't seem to be any *meaning* to any of it.

At Montvale, Abby had a busy life. She had charitable work, and she took care of their tenants. She had even been responsible for the building of a village school for the local children to attend.

Alison wanted a life like that.

A life where she could fill her days doing good for people and come home at night to a loving husband.

Captain Sorrell had escorted her back to their box and then left to procure refreshments.

As the evening wore on, the place was growing more raucous.

When Alison entered the box, she was surprised to see Lord Fulham sitting close to Harriet, their heads bent together.

He looked up then and his eyes raked her, gleaming with obvious admiration.

"Good evening, Miss Langton." He stood and bowed over her hand, placing a kiss on the back of it.

Alison resisted the urge to snatch the limb back from him.

"Good evening, Lord Fulham. What a surprise to find you here."

His smile didn't quiet reach his eyes as he stepped closer to her.

"A pleasant surprise I hope, my dear Miss Langton?"

"Of course." She smiled politely.

He didn't say anything else, so Alison cast around for a topic of discussion.

"Are you enjoying your evening, my lord?" she asked.

"I always enjoy a trip to Vauxhall Gardens," Lord

Fulham said, casting his eye around the revellers outside. "So decadent. So much to see."

"I'm quite in awe of it," she confessed. "I've never seen anything like it."

"And have you visited the ruins and the fountains?"

Alison shook her head. "Not yet," she said. "I expect that we will, once Captain Billings and Captain Sorrell have returned."

"Oh, but there isn't a moment to waste." He smiled charmingly. "You simply must see the tightrope walkers above the pathways. And you want to return to your box in time for the fireworks, do you not?"

"Most definitely," she said quickly. She was desperate to see the fireworks, and the tightrope walkers sounded thrilling. "Perhaps Miss Billings and I could –"

"Why don't I escort you to see them, Miss Langton?" he continued smoothly. "I will ensure that no harm befalls you. It wouldn't be safe for two young ladies to wander out there alone. Things can get quite – er – *lively* at times."

She could well imagine what he meant.

Even now, ladies and gentlemen of both classes were stumbling about. And the goings on in some of the boxes around them were nothing short of alarming.

She so badly wanted to see it all. But this was Lord Fulham. Lord Fulham who had all the appearance of being enamoured of Harriet at the musicale and only moments prior. Not to mention James and Rob really, truly didn't want her to spend time in his company.

Nicholas didn't want her with him, either.

The thought of Nicholas made her gut twist with hurt and a feeling of stubbornness to awake inside of her.

Lord Fulham had always been so attentive to her. Unlike that gentleman, who'd been occupying far too many of her thoughts.

Her mind made up, Alison beamed at the man, ignoring her misgivings about his flirtations with her friend, and the dire warnings from her guardians.

"That would be lovely, thank you, my lord."

His light blue eyes lit with a triumphant gleam, and Alison wondered if she were making a mistake.

If Robert were to find out that she'd wandered off with a gentleman with whom she hadn't arrived, and who he had forbidden her to spend time with, he'd have her head.

But then, she reasoned, Robert wasn't here.

And Lord Fulham had never been anything but kind and charming to her.

Besides, she would take Harriet along.

She looked over at her friend, shocked to see her drinking wine from a goblet held to her lips by a man she hadn't even noticed come into the box.

"My friend, Lord Severill," Lord Fulham said. "He will take care of Miss Billings. Now, shall we?"

Alison felt a stirring of trepidation. The name Severill was familiar to her, she was sure.

She wasn't at all sure, however, that this was a good idea.

However, another glance at Harriet told her she didn't particularly want to be in their box at that time, either.

Who would have thought that quiet, unassuming Miss Billings would be so – well, so *scandalous?*

Alison was uncomfortable enough she decided to leave with Lord Fulham despite her concerns.

She would take a quick walk and return when she was sure Captain Billings would be back to take them home. Besides, she didn't particularly want to be present when the captain returned and saw his sister like that.

So, squashing down all her misgivings, she took the arm Lord Fulham extended and allowed him to lead her away from the crowds.

THE PLEASURE GARDENS had reached the point where inhibitions were well and truly thrown to the wind by the time Nic marched inside.

He was neither surprised nor bothered when Robert showed up behind him only minutes later.

They had made short work of purchasing tickets, and now they were inside. And faced with absolute chaos.

"I'm assuming they've procured a box?" Nic asked shortly.

The chances were slim, he knew, that any harm would come to Alison.

But equally he knew he would be unable to relax until he had her safe and well, if not in his arms, then at least in his line of vision.

They hurried to where the boxes were located, Nic's eyes darting around people more foxed than not.

"Billings!"

Nic whipped around at the sound of Robert's shout in time to see two scarlet-coated officers rush toward them, a tearful young lady in between them.

"Y-your grace," one of the young captains, Billings presumably, was gasping.

"Where is Miss Langton?"

Nic hadn't even been introduced to the man before him, yet he was beyond caring.

The slighter man's eyes darted from Robert to Nic.

"S-she went for a walk, Mister?"

"The Duke of Barnbury," he snapped, watching with grim amusement as the man's eyes widened. "A walk?"

"Y-yes, your grace. I came back to the box, and my sister –" He turned a glare on the sniffling young lady. "Was in the company of Lord Severill."

Nic's stomach dropped, and he shared a frown with Robert.

Last year, Simon had nearly killed Severill with his bare hands when the man had attacked Amelia on the balcony of Dashford Manor.

He was a bastard, and so were the men whose company he kept.

Nic felt a snake of fear slither through his veins.

"And Miss Langton?" he prompted.

Something of what he was feeling must have shown on his face, for the young man paled significantly.

"Harriet?" He nudged the snivelling debutante, who glanced up briefly at Nic and Rob before dropping her eyes to her feet.

"She went for a walk as my brother said," she mumbled.

"Alone?" Rob bit out.

"N-no, your grace." She sniffed before raising tear-filled eyes once more to Robert. "With Lord Fulham."

Nic didn't even stay to hear what Rob said to the group.

He turned and darted toward the maze of darkened walkways and corners.

He knew exactly where a blackguard like Fulham would go.

Somewhere dark and isolated, where Alison would be vulnerable.

He told himself over and over that she would be fine.

If only he could believe it.

Chapter Seventeen

"I REALLY WOULD prefer to turn back now, my lord."

Alison dug her heels in, refusing to let Lord Fulham pull her further into the darkened maze of pathways.

The tightrope walkers had been wonderful, just as he'd said.

However, she noticed that the crowd of people was getting scarcer, and she wasn't willing to put herself in any sort of danger.

"But there is so much more to see, Miss Langton." He smiled but instead of finding it charming this time, Alison just found it unnerving.

She had been foolish to come out here with him. She knew that.

So desperate had she been to escape Harriet's behaviour, to be distracted from her thoughts of Nicholas, that she'd ignored all the warnings in her gut and rushed out here with him.

"There is the most beautiful fountain just up ahead," he said now. "It is truly a sight to behold. It would be a shame for you to miss it."

He tugged on her arm, forcing her to stumble a few steps forward.

"I'd really rather not, Lord Fulham," she said through gritted teeth, pulling herself from his grip.

"You'll regret missing it, my dear," he insisted.

"And you'll regret not taking your damned hands off her!"

Alison and Fulham both turned at the sound of the voice behind them.

There stood Nic, looking coldly furious.

Alison shivered at the look in his eye.

Though she had never feared him, and never would, she could sense the power from him and knew he would intimidate even the bravest of men.

Fulham, it turned out, was a coward.

"I didn't touch her," he said straightaway, stepping back and holding his hands up.

The smile on Nic's face was both beautiful and terrifying.

"And nor will you," he promised, deathly quiet.

"The lady wanted to see the –"

"Perhaps I haven't made myself clear."

Nicholas stepped forward, and even Alison stepped away from the look of fury in his eyes.

"I don't care what the lady wanted or didn't want. I don't care what you did or didn't do." He stepped closer still, his voice low and deceptively calm, and all the more terrifying for it. "If I see you anywhere near her again, I'll tear you apart with my bare hands. Understand?"

Alison's jaw dropped and though she felt a flicker of irritation that he should ignore her for three days and then act like a jealous suitor, she didn't think now would be the best time to mention such a thing.

For one thing, he was ferociously angry. For another, she very much wanted Lord Fulham to stay away from her.

Fulham darted a look between Alison and Nicholas before turning and without another word, hurrying back toward the boxes.

The relief Alison felt was overwhelmed only by the joy of being with Nicholas again.

Even though she'd been hurt that he'd disappeared, the fact that he'd shown up here when she needed someone like a knight in shining armour melted her heart.

She turned her gaze up to him, preparing to thank him.

But his face was still stony, his eyes lit with unholy fire.

Her words died in her throat as she got caught in the intensity of that expression.

He had yet to move, yet to speak. And the silence was becoming unbearable.

"Nicholas, I –"

Just those two, innocuous words seemed to un-freeze him, and he suddenly reached out, wrapping his hands around her upper arms.

She didn't have time to feel ecstatic at the feel of his touch before he glared down at her.

"What the hell is wrong with you?" he asked, and any thought of thanks or gratitude quickly fled as anger sparked hot and potent inside her.

NIC SAW THE exact moment that relief and tenderness left her deep, blue gaze to be replaced by a raw, fiery anger.

"What's wrong with *me?*" she screeched, and he resisted the urge to flinch.

Now that he had his hands on her, his heart had stopped thundering so much. It still thumped erratical-ly, but for a véry different reason.

He wouldn't, however, focus on the floral scent of her, or how mesmerising her eyes were when sparked with fury.

He wouldn't be distracted by that mouth, open now, no doubt, to blister his ears.

And he wouldn't, absolutely wouldn't pull her against him just to feel her body pressed to his. Just to feel that she was here with him. Safe.

"You have some nerve, your grace, ignoring me for

days and then swooping in here, acting as though you have the right to control what I do and with whom."

"Did you *want* to be dragged down a dark pathway by a creature such as Fulham?" he bit back, his temper igniting once more. "Do you have any idea what could have happened to you? Even coming to a place like this without proper supervision is dangerous and fool-hardy."

"Oh, for goodness sake."

She dragged herself away from his hold, and he knew he was every sort of fool for missing the feel of her in his arms.

"I was well supervised by Harriet's brother," she said, scowling at his raised brow.

Did she just growl?

"I might have been a little – hasty in allowing Lord Fulham to walk with me."

He snorted derisively, earning another scowl.

She was quite beautiful when angry. Something else he felt it best not to say.

"But I wanted to see the gardens. I wanted to see the fountains, and the tightropes, and the fireworks. And you would know all that if you hadn't run away and ignored me after we spent such a lovely afternoon together."

Nic was starting to calm down now, and he felt the beginnings of a twinge of guilt prickle at his con-science.

Once again, fear of his own heart had hurt her.

"It was still completely irresponsible to come down here with him."

Her jaw dropped, and she stamped her foot like a child before turning, her white skirts swirling about her feet, and marched off further down the pathway.

"Alison!" he called after her, but she ignored him.

With a sigh and a prayer for patience, Nic went after her.

He found her standing near an ornate fountain surrounded by low hanging trees, benches half-hidden against their branches.

This, Nic thought, was the perfect place for an assignation. He almost groaned aloud at the desire that unfurled in him at the idea.

Not the time, Nic, he told himself firmly.

"Alison –"

He didn't get a chance to finish whatever he'd been about to say.

She swirled around, hands planted on her hips, glaring up at him.

"You are an overbearing, controlling, joyless *bore,*" she yelled at him.

She was in a towering rage.

He probably deserved it, but he couldn't help but feel a bit affronted at her less-than-complimentary opinion of him.

"You stand there in judgment of everyone and

everything that doesn't live up to your lofty expectations," she continued, really getting into her stride now. "And nobody ever *could*."

He stepped forward, hating the hurt lurking behind the anger.

"If you just –"

"Don't you ever tire of being so *responsible* all the time?" she continued, uncaring about his attempts to interrupt her tirade. "So bloody saintly?"

He was shocked to hear her swear.

And he really shouldn't find it arousing. He knew that. Of course, he knew it.

"Don't you ever want to break the rules? Sin just a little?"

It snapped.

The last vestige of his celebrated self-control snapped.

"Hell, yes," he responded before pulling her against him and capturing her mouth in a searing kiss.

Chapter Eighteen

ALISON FROZE IN utter shock for a millisecond before she went up in flames.

For so long she had dreamed of being kissed by him.

Never could she have imagined it would feel like this.

Like she burned with a raging fire he awoke in her.

The fact that she had thought they'd kissed on Simon's balcony a year ago was laughable. That had been no kiss, not if this was anything to go by.

She gasped at the onslaught of feeling, and his tongue delved inside her mouth, coaxing hers to dance with his own.

Her knees buckled, and she reached up to cling desperately to the lapels of his coat as his arms wrapped around her waist and pulled her impossibly close to the rock-hard length of him.

Alison didn't know how long the kiss went on for. It felt like seconds and eons.

This was beyond anything she'd ever experienced, and she wasn't sure how much she could withstand.

The heart that had been desperately trying to fly to him for weeks burst with a love so strong, so intense, that her whole world shifted on its axis.

The kiss went on and on, and she never wanted it to end.

His hands were everywhere. Holding her face, moving to her hair, then burning a trail over her back, her hips, pulling her closer still.

Her own had moved as if of their own accord to plunge into his chestnut hair.

She could die happy right here, right now.

He pulled his lips suddenly from her own but before she could protest, he moved to press them against the rapidly beating pulse at her throat.

Alison moaned in tortured pleasure as he trailed kisses across her neck, moved to bite gently on her ear.

"Nicholas," she gasped, pleading for something she didn't even understand.

"Nicholas."

The sound of Robert's voice suddenly sounded from down the pathway, and Nicholas sprang back from Alison as though scalded.

She stared at him, her breathing as laboured as his own appeared to be.

Lord, but he looked handsome. His hair was mussed, and his navy eyes were so heated she felt them scorch her even from a distance.

"I –"

Whatever he'd been about to say was cut off by the sudden appearance of Robert, whose wintry grey eyes moved slowly between them, his face stoic.

"You found her then," he said softly.

As Alison watched, the two gentlemen stared at each other intently.

It was as though they were communicating without speaking a word.

Finally, after a tense few moments, Robert nodded and turned his gaze to Alison.

"You're well?" he asked softly, and she couldn't tell if he were angry with her or not.

She didn't trust herself to speak. Not after that kiss. Not with the tumultuous emotions still swirling inside her.

Instead of attempting it, she merely nodded her head, feeling the hair loosened by Nicholas's hands begin to fall from its pins.

She felt her cheeks heat as Robert's eyes flicked to the blonde strands, then back to her face.

"Perhaps it's time to return home, hmm?"

He held an arm out and she hurried to take it, afraid to look at Nicholas let alone speak to him.

"I came here on Dante," Robert said, turning his gaze to Nicholas. "Alison will have to return in your carriage."

Her heart flew into her mouth at Robert's words.

She wasn't sure if that were a good thing or not.

Nicholas had yet to even speak to Robert, let alone her.

"Of course," he suddenly said, hoarsely. "I'll –"

"You'll ride Dante," Robert interrupted smoothly. "And I'll be taking your carriage."

There was another tension-filled look between the gentlemen, and Alison willed Nicholas to refuse. To say he wanted to travel back with her.

But, of course, he was Saint Nicholas. He would never do that, even if he had just kissed the living daylights out of her.

"Come, Alison." Robert's tone brooked no argument, and she biddably hurried up the pathway, her hand ensconced in his arm.

Nicholas trailed behind them.

Though silent, she could feel his presence every step of the way.

NICHOLAS'S HEART THUMPED painfully as he rode Dante home through the streets of London.

It was busy with members of the *haute monde* coming home from various events, and gentlemen heading away from Mayfair to indulge their proclivities.

Nicholas barely saw any of it.

He couldn't concentrate on the sights and sounds around him.

He couldn't think about anything but her.

The feel of her. The scent of her.

The taste of her.

Damn it.

Nic groaned aloud as his mind replayed in vivid detail every second of their embrace.

To call it a mere kiss would be inaccurate.

He had known that if he let his control slip, if he risked tasting her, just once, that it would be explosive.

But never could he have imagined the effect it would have had.

The second his lips had touched her own, the world shifted beneath his feet. What he had felt went beyond desire. Beyond lust. Beyond attraction.

It was so much more than all of that. And so much more frightening than he'd suspected it would be. Because now he knew that he would crave her with every single fibre of his being for the rest of his life.

He shouldn't have let Robert take her away.

He shouldn't have stood there in silence while she glanced back at him, her blue eyes filled with confusion, whilst Robert handed her into Nic's carriage.

But what else could he have done?

Alison was an innocent. But Nicholas, though she called him saintly, was not. And neither was Robert.

Robert knew exactly what had happened at that fountain, and Nic wouldn't insult the man's intelligence by lying about it.

So where did that leave him?

If it had been anyone but Robert who'd walked down that pathway, Nic's hand would have been forced.

They would have been made to marry.

The burst of elation that shot through him at the thought was frightening but now, he had to admit to himself, not wholly unexpected.

His heart knew what his mind refused to acknowledge.

But it had been Robert. And Robert would never force Nic or Alison to do anything.

Nicholas's head spun until he felt nauseated.

What the hell was he going to do?

Now that there was some distance between them, he found it easier to remember all the reasons he didn't want to marry. All the reasons he didn't want to be responsible for someone else's happiness, not in such an intimate way. Not in any way beyond the good he did in St. Giles.

More importantly, he was able to remember why he and Alison were so unsuited.

His quiet, unassuming life would no doubt be boring to her.

And though she loved her family fiercely and was kind to everyone she met, he couldn't imagine her being involved in any real way with the work he did in St. Giles. And he wouldn't want her anywhere near the

178

place anyway.

He spent so much time there, was so heavily involved in it. And he didn't want to give it up. It was the only thing that kept the guilt away. That and blocking out as many emotions and feelings as he could.

Alison – well, Alison brought fierce, unstoppable, life-changing emotions to the surface just by being in the same room as him.

And he knew that if she were his, truly his, he wouldn't want to be away from her long enough to continue his work.

If he let her, she would consume every single part of him.

So, he couldn't let her.

They wouldn't suit.

This thing between them couldn't go anywhere, and that was final.

Upon reaching his house, he summoned a footman to take Dante back to Robert's.

He knew that he and Robert had a reckoning coming, but he couldn't face the confrontation tonight.

Robert would want an answer, and Nic couldn't think of one to give him.

Not when he was consumed by her.

Not when he knew it would mean losing her forever.

Chapter Nineteen

ALL MORNING, ALISON had sat in the window of the drawing room, watching the road outside.

She could see Nicholas's house from here.

See when he left.

If he would come here.

She hadn't slept a wink last night, and she was grouchy. She knew it, and Abigail knew it, too, for she had left Alison at home while visiting Senna.

Amelia was going to join the ladies at James's house that morning, and Alison should be there, as well.

Senna was her cousin through marriage, after all. And Lottie would be there, along with Poppy.

The ladies would all enjoy a comfortable coze and spend a wonderful morning together. Poppy would entertain them, and they could all coo over Lottie and talk excitedly about Senna's baby.

And Alison would miss it all. A fact that she felt particularly guilty over since she'd barely seen Senna and Amelia outside of evening events, given that she tended to spend her days obsessing about the brooding duke with whom she'd fallen desperately in love.

Like an idiot.

The ride home last night with Robert had been excruciating.

He hadn't asked her what had gone on between her and Nicholas.

He'd questioned her about Captain Billings, and ultimately been satisfied the man had done his best to take care of her.

Then he'd questioned her about Lord Fulham, which hadn't gone well at all.

After he'd vocalised a couple of alarmingly descriptive ways to damage the man, he'd warned her firmly that she weren't to so much as glance in his direction again.

Try as she might to explain that Lord Fulham hadn't actually *done* anything inappropriate, it fell on deaf ears.

Robert was as fond of the young viscount as Nicholas appeared to be.

Robert needn't worry in any case. She doubted very much that Lord Fulham would want anything to do with her now. There wasn't a man alive who could stand up to the considerable power of two dukes. Especially those two.

And when James found out, he'd probably blister her ears, as well.

But when it came to Nicholas, Robert hadn't said a

word.

Not a single word.

Robert had handed her out of the carriage, sent the driver back to Nicholas's, and once inside, had said his goodnights and disappeared.

This morning at breakfast, he'd been his usual self. And though Abigail had questioned her about the evening, it was obvious Robert hadn't said anything about how he'd found Alison and Nicholas together.

With only a brief word of caution about Lord Fulham, and a suggestion that perhaps Harriet Billings wasn't the best choice of friend, a sentiment with which Alison whole-heartedly agreed, Abigail had moved the conversation along.

Alison had frowned in confusion but when she'd caught Robert's eye, she knew to stay quiet.

Abigail soon left the table to ready Lottie for their visit to Senna's, and Robert causally announced that he would accompany them, saying that he needed to speak to James.

Alison's stomach had flipped uneasily but Robert didn't seem at all sombre, or that he were going over there to discuss anything serious.

Perhaps, she told herself rather unconvincingly, *he didn't notice anything unusual last night. Perhaps it didn't look as obvious as I feared.*

But it was no use.

She would worry about it until she saw them all

together and could see with her own eyes that she hadn't ruined their friendship or forced Nicholas's hand, if Robert and James decided to insist that they marry.

Nothing in the world would mean more to Alison than becoming Nic's wife.

But not like that. Not because he was forced to do it. Not because honour would dictate that he protect her reputation.

She loved him far too much to confine him to a life with her if he did not love her.

And given that he hadn't called today, he was making his feelings fairly clear.

But could he truly have kissed her like that, held her like that, if he felt nothing?

A sudden movement at Nicholas's house distracted Alison from her maudlin thoughts.

And there he was.

Her breath caught in her throat as she watched him descend the steps of his house toward a waiting carriage.

He was so handsome it made her heart ache.

His superfine jacket was a dark, rich blue, only shades lighter than his eyes.

And now she knew for sure that it wasn't padded; that the broad shoulders and large upper arms were all him.

She watched until one shiny Hessian disappeared

into the carriage, wondering where he was off to.

A servant hurried toward him, and he turned from entering the conveyance to converse with the footman.

She didn't think he'd go to James's today.

Not unless he'd been summoned.

Her stomach twisted uneasily once again at the thought and suddenly, she was on her feet.

Robert would have her head for what she was about to do.

Dashing up the stairs to her bedchamber, Alison grabbed her reticule, which always contained some of her pin money, a light pelisse in a shade of dusky pink that matched the ribbon on her white gown, and a straw bonnet with a sprig of pink and white flowers, and turned to run full pelt back down the stairs.

She threw open the front door, not even waiting for the footman to do it, and ran out to the street.

Nicholas's carriage had only just set off, the footman who'd delayed him just now returning to the house.

She hurried quickly down the street, aware of the looks she was receiving given she didn't even have a maid with her.

Robert and James would probably lock her in a tower after this.

With her heart thumping furiously, Alison rushed to the top of the busy street. As she hoped, she spotted a hackney.

Without pausing to check that she wasn't recognised getting into it, she dove inside and instructed the driver to head in the same direction as Nicholas's carriage, pointing out the rather helpful crest of Barnbury on the side of the black lacquered coach.

He was going to face Robert and James, or he was going on one of his mysterious trips that nobody ever seemed to know about.

Either way, she was going to find out what he was up to.

She sat back, willing her heart to cease its thundering.

There were worse things in the world, she assured herself, than a woman travelling by herself.

Glancing out the rather dirty window of the hack, she was both alarmed and relieved to see that they were travelling in the opposite direction to James's house.

In fact, they seemed to be leaving Mayfair altogether.

Curious now, Alison kept her eyes on the streets outside, trepidation starting to form as they grew murkier, the buildings more dilapidated, the people certainly not the polished and pristine Peerage.

Lords and ladies gave way first to merchants and shopkeepers, but then even they seemed to drop away.

They had entered a part of London that Alison wasn't familiar with, and given the stench beginning to permeate the carriage, she wasn't sure she wanted to be.

Though there had been one or two areas that didn't look half so bad as where she was now; the buildings clean, the streets adequately paved, and even obviously wealthy gentlemen milling around them, for the most part, this place was truly deplorable.

The slums, because to call them buildings would be a gross exaggeration, seemed to be toppling over onto one another, and she could barely tell where one ended and the other began.

To her horror, she saw tiny, filthy children darting in and out of them and concluded that these shacks must be where they lived.

The streets were littered with people half-starved and barely moving, the ground sludgy with something she couldn't even bring herself to contemplate.

These were the dregs of society. The poorest of the poor. And Alison's heart ached for every soul she gazed upon.

How could people live like this? So close yet so vastly far from where she, herself, lived in grandeur and luxury?

It didn't seem fair. It *wasn't* fair.

Alison was so distracted by her maudlin musings that she didn't even feel the carriage coming to a halt.

"'Ere ye are, Miss."

She snapped her gaze to the driver then looked out to see that they'd come to a stop in front of a surprisingly clean and pleasant-looking building.

This one was clean and well-maintained, with three stories of windows and a sturdy-looking roof.

"Th-this is where the carriage came to?"

"Just gone round the back, Miss," the driver confirmed, nodding toward a wide alleyway by the side of the building.

"Do you know what this is?" she asked, hoping against hope that it wasn't a brothel or something equally scandalous.

Her heart would break at the mere thought that Nicholas could have gone from kissing her last night to –

"Oi haven't a clue, Miss. You just told me to follow the carriage, and Oi did."

Alison was alarmed as an impatient edge entered the driver's tone.

She didn't want to leave the relative safety of the hack, but she had a feeling if she didn't leave of her own accord, or tell him to turn immediately back around, she'd be tossed out regardless.

Self-preservation warred with curiosity.

"Miss?"

Alison took a deep breath, trying not to gag at the stench of rot and filth filling her lungs.

"Th-thank you."

She pressed a guinea into his soiled glove and stepped out of the hackney.

Stumbling slightly at the rather large drop from the carriage to the ground, she righted herself and glanced around her.

Her stomach dropped as she swiftly gained the attention of more than one hostile-looking person, and fear snaked its way around her heart.

I shouldn't have come, she thought a little hysterically.

There were only steps between where she stood and the front of the building into which Nicholas had apparently disappeared, but it suddenly felt like miles.

From the corner of her eye, Alison saw a man, caked in dirt and staggering slightly, begin to move toward her.

Without hesitation, she darted toward the building.

Whatever she was going to find in there, she could only hope that it would be safer than the streets.

Chapter Twenty

"AND HOW ARE John and Bonnie doing now?" Nic was finishing up a meeting with Mrs. Cafferty, which should have held all his attention.

But instead, inevitably, his mind was elsewhere.

On a pair of blue eyes that he couldn't stop thinking about and a mouth that had kept him awake all last night.

"Bonnie is doing right as rain, your grace." The older lady smiled.

"And John?"

Here, her face fell.

"It's different for him, I think," she began carefully, "He's older. He remembers things that, God willing, Bonnie has forgotten. It will take him some time. He's skittish. Won't let anyone near him."

Nic frowned.

The problem with boys like John wasn't that they weren't trusting. God knew they had no reason to be.

But sometimes they were bolters. And Nic couldn't be sure that he would find him again if he did take off.

The idea of losing a child he was trying to save

filled him with horror.

"How are his studies?"

Mrs. Cafferty sighed.

"Again, your grace, it's not that the child hasn't a brain in his head. But he won't let nobody help him. Bonnie is doing well with her letters and numbers, though."

Nic nodded.

"I'm sure she'd love to see you. All of the children would."

Seeing Bonnie would be yet another reason to think of nothing but Alison Langton, Nic knew. But he always called in to see the children when he came here, and today would be no different.

After all, he couldn't stop thinking about Alison anyway. He might as well visit with the children. If anything were going to distract him from Alison, it would be them.

He wandered to the schoolrooms. At this time of day, the tutors Nic paid for would have small groups of children in various rooms teaching them to read, write, and for the more able, history and the sciences.

Nic's goal was to give the children a good education and then, when they were older, help them to procure good, honest work with a steady income and a dependable roof over their heads.

A lot of them ended up on his various estates.

The groups were kept purposely small.

When the children came to them, they didn't do particularly well in big groups.

And none of them were ever forced to take part in any of the lessons.

Gradual coaxing worked better.

All the children who came here had suffered abuse at the hands of adults. Some worse than others. Some so unspeakable that Nic couldn't allow himself to think of it.

"Bonnie and John will be in the yellow playroom," Mrs. Cafferty said referring to one of the many bright, airy rooms filled with toys and books. "John doesn't want to join lessons yet, and Bonnie won't leave him. We send a tutor in every morning to help them both."

Nic nodded, frowning in concern.

"Do they spend much time out of doors?" he asked.

"When we can spare someone to take them," Mrs. Cafferty responded. "They're not mixing too well with the other children just yet. There's nobody free this afternoon, but we'll make sure that they go outside tomorrow."

Just like the playrooms and classrooms, the garden outside had been designed with children in mind. There was a rockery and trees for them to climb, ponds to study fish and frogs in. Gardens with vegetable and flower beds where they could learn to grow their own food, and in the middle, a fountain for them to paddle in during summer months.

Upon reaching the door of the yellow room, Nic pushed it open.

It was empty.

He turned to question Mrs. Cafferty and saw the woman's face blanch.

"Where are they?" he asked, his voice stamped with concern.

"I-I don't know," she gasped. "They were right here, your grace. I –"

A maid appeared at the end of the corridor, and Mrs. Cafferty called out to her. "Lizzie, have you seen Bonnie and John?"

The maid blinked in shock, no doubt surprised at the usually affable Mrs. Cafferty sounding so severe.

"Yes, ma'am," she answered, bobbing a curtsy to Nic. "The young lady took them outside. Bonnie was of a mind to look at the fish."

"What young lady?" Nic barked, feeling guilty when the young girl's face paled. "My apologies, Lizzie, is it?" he asked.

The maids here were just like everyone else; the gardeners, the cook and her helpers, the burly footmen. All born and raised on the streets. All helped by Nicholas and his various charities.

"Y-yes, your grace," she stammered.

"What young lady took them?" He kept his tone calm and steady.

Bonnie and John wouldn't be the first children to

have been born to a prostitute or to end up with someone who would use them for ill purposes. Evil purposes, a lot of the time.

If someone had come to take them back to wherever they'd come from…

"Your friend, your grace," Lizzie said, confusing him all the more.

His friend?

Who would –?

No! It couldn't be.

Nobody knew of the amount of time Nic personally spent here. They were aware of his charitable endeavours but believed he gave his money and not his time and attention to his causes.

And he had no friends from St. Giles that didn't work in one of his charities.

The only way someone would know he was here would be if they'd seen him come in.

And only one person, one irritating, hoydenish tearaway would be foolish enough, and courageous enough, and uncaring about flouting the rules of Society enough to follow him into the depth of St. Giles.

But surely the fates wouldn't be so cruel?

"Miss Langton, your grace."

And apparently the fates were exactly that cruel.

She'd followed him?

She'd bloody well come to St. Giles alone?

A fear unlike any he'd experienced in years at what could have happened to her exploded inside him and set his feet in motion before the maid had finished speaking. He had to see for himself that Alison was well.

Then he could decide whether he wanted to kiss her or wring her foolish neck.

Nic burst into the gardens, Mrs. Cafferty huffing and puffing behind him.

He darted his gaze around, spotting a glimpse of bright, golden hair by the fountain.

He moved toward it, his heart thundering at what might have been.

Getting ready to ring a peal over her beautiful, foolish head, Nic came to an abrupt halt and took in the scene before him, jaw open in shock.

Bonnie was splashing about the fountain, squealing and giggling to her heart's content.

As usual, John was standing to the side, watching with sullen, mistrustful eyes.

And Alison – Alison was standing between them both, bedecked in white and pink, a breath of fresh air and purity in a world so filled with misery and depravity.

She reminded him once again of an angel as she laughed at Bonnie's splashing, the sound like a melody ringing out across the gardens.

Alison was getting splashed – her hair, her face. Nic

swallowed past a sudden lump in his throat.

Even the front of her gown.

He thanked God for her pelisse because he wasn't entirely sure he'd be able to control himself if it wasn't covering her.

He didn't know a single woman of Quality who wouldn't be horrified by a street urchin ruining an expensive gown, wetting her perfectly coiffed hair.

Yet, there she stood, uncaring about it all.

Nic had intended to march over there and after making sure there wasn't a hair on her head hurt, giving her the set down she obviously needed.

Had she no care for her safety?

Had she any idea what lurked in these streets morning, noon, and night?

Anything could have happened.

He could have walked out of here and found her body, lifeless on the street.

Just like –

No. He wouldn't think it. Couldn't think it.

All intentions of yelling at her flew from his mind. He stood frozen. Mesmerised.

Bonnie ran over and threw her arms around Alison, well and truly soaking her.

But instead of shying away, Alison lifted the child into a cuddle Nic was sure she had rarely received in her short life.

With their heads bent together, they looked so

alike. Alison could be her mother.

And Nic's heart pounded for a very different reason.

After a whispered conversation, they both turned to look at John.

He was gazing at them both. A mixture of longing and defiance in his young eyes.

"Should we take the children, your grace?" Mrs. Cafferty, whom Nic had quite forgotten about, spoke in soft tones, apparently as unwilling to let the occupants of the garden know of their presence as Nic was himself.

He merely shook his head, not trusting himself to speak.

As he watched, Alison put Bonnie carefully back in the low-walled fountain and moved toward John.

The child glared up at her, but she continued, hunkering in front of him when she was close.

They spoke for a moment or two and Nic could tell, even from here, that John wasn't giving much more than one-word answers.

Alison pointed to the fountain, earning a stubborn shake of his head.

Nic was about to step in, afraid that John would run off, when suddenly, Alison sat on the ground proving once and for all that she was very much unconcerned about her dress.

He watched, couldn't tear his eyes away, as she

reached down and pulled off her kid boots.

Surely she wasn't doing what he thought she was doing.

The devil himself couldn't have dragged Nic's gaze away from her as she reached under her skirts and pulled off her stockings.

Nic had seen women naked from the time he'd been a lad.

Never had any of them affected him as much as seeing Alison Langton's calves.

It took every bit of strength he had not to groan aloud at the sight of legs that would haunt him now just as much as her kiss.

She stood and hitched her skirts up to her knees, striding forward and, without hesitating, stepping into the fountain alongside Bonnie, laughing at the child's cry of delight.

Hell and damnation, he thought. *She'll be the death of me.*

Chapter Twenty-One

I F ANYONE FROM the *ton* saw her now, she would be well and truly ruined.

But Alison grinned as the adorable little girl, so like Poppy, kicked water in the air, well and truly destroying her dress.

That would take some explaining, she knew.

She watched Bonnie's brother, John, out of the corner of her eye.

He had taken a few hesitant steps forward. But Alison sensed even that was hard for the poor boy.

When she'd burst through the front door of this place only two hours ago, never would she have imagined that this is what she'd find.

It was hard to believe that such a frightening, dismal place lurked beyond these walls.

Even the air seemed cleaner in this secluded garden. So filled was it with the scent of flowers and apples from the small orchard in the corner.

It was like a little spot of Heaven, right in the middle of Hell.

The whole place was incredible.

She'd run up the steps to the front door, hammering on it in her panic.

It had been opened by a burly footman who had glared at her, his eyes suspicious and unforgiving.

"I-I'm a friend of his grace, the Duke of Barnbury," she'd gasped, still unaware of what she'd find but hoping it would be safer than outside.

The man's eyes had widened as she spoke then raked over her clothing before stepping back and allowing her entrance.

Alison had been amazed.

She was standing in a bright, sunny entrance, spotlessly clean and filled with solid, good quality furniture.

She'd gazed around open-mouthed, sure that it wasn't a brothel or a gambling hell.

The arrival of a young lady, not in anything scandalous but in a clean, serviceable grey gown and apron confirmed that this couldn't be any place sinful.

"Can I help you, Miss?" She had bobbed a curtsy, staring curiously at Alison.

"Miss Langton," Alison finally said. "I am acquainted with the Duke of Barnbury. I –"

"Oh, you are one of our patronesses?" The maid smiled kindly. "You've not come alone, have you Miss?"

"Um – m-my maid took ill. So, I sent her home."

It had been as poor an excuse as any she'd ever thought of, but it was the best she could do on the spot.

Whether the young maid, Lizzie, had believed her or not, Alison didn't know.

Thankfully, she hadn't pried any further.

"What *is* this place?" Alison had asked.

Lizzie had launched into an explanation of the incredible work they did here, showing her around the rooms, introducing her to the children.

A relief unlike any she'd ever known had swept through Alison. *This* was the reason he came to St. Giles all the time. It wasn't depravity or gambling. It was to help those less fortunate.

The tour brought her to the schoolrooms, and that was how she'd come across Bonnie and her untrusting brother, alone in a beautiful room. Bonnie had been looking out the window; John was sitting with his arms crossed, scowling at nothing.

It had taken some doing, but she'd managed to coax John out into the garden, claiming she wanted to see them but didn't feel entirely safe without a male escort.

As she'd guessed, the boy had an innate instinct to protect, and he'd grudgingly agreed to accompany Alison and Bonnie.

Now, she hoped that by making a spectacle of herself, John would be convinced to join the fun in the water.

He was just a boy. He deserved to have some childish fun.

She didn't press him or force him.

Instead, she played with Bonnie and gave him some space.

Alison had her back to where John had been standing when she heard the distinctive splash of a pair of feet.

Her heart raced as she turned slowly, trying to appear nonchalant.

To her elation, John was standing in the water, his charcoal breeches rolled up to the knee.

She grinned at him and was thrilled when he grinned back.

She opened her mouth to say something when he suddenly kicked out, covering her in a deluge of water.

She gasped in shock as it hit her square in the face.

They stared at each other for a moment before Alison burst into peals of laughter.

The sound of John's laugh merging with her own made her happier than she could ever remember being.

Alison had no idea how long she stayed in that fountain, she and Bonnie squealing as John chased them round and round, all of them splashing as they went.

She hoped the children were allowed to play in it but reasoned that they must be.

Everything here seemed so well thought out, so child-centred, that it would be foolish to have it so accessible if it weren't intended for them to enjoy.

Besides, even if she got into trouble, it would be worth it to see the siblings laugh and play.

Eventually, Bonnie's teeth began to chatter, and Alison wondered aloud if they should end their game.

The sound of a bell, however, drowned out her question.

"It's dinner time!" Bonnie exclaimed and jumped out of the fountain and toward her shoes.

They hadn't thought about drying off, so Alison used a dry patch of her gown to dry their feet as best she could before helping Bonnie with her shoes.

Finally, the children had shoes on, and she sent them in ahead of her, afraid that they'd get into trouble if she kept them late.

She didn't know how strict this Mrs. Cafferty they told her of was. Though Bonnie, at least, sounded as though she liked the woman well enough.

Alison bent to pick up her stockings and boots, knowing there was no way she could put them back on, being as wet and bedraggled as she was.

Shrugging her shoulders in defeat, Alison turned around, and straight into a rock solid something.

Gasping in surprise, she looked up.

Right into the face of Nicholas Fyfe.

And he did not look happy.

IF NIC LIVED to be a hundred years old, nothing would ever surprise him as much as watching Alison Langton destroy her clothes and play in a fountain with two orphans from the streets of St. Giles.

He reached his arms out to steady her as she stumbled back.

She gazed up at him, her eyes the colour of cornflowers in the summer sun, her hair wet and plastered to her face.

He'd sent Mrs. Cafferty inside with Bonnie and John, being careful not to show how pleased he'd been to see John join in the game.

How had Alison done it?

In one short afternoon she'd engaged John in a way nobody else had been able to.

It would appear Nicholas wasn't the only one susceptible to the little enchantress.

There was so much he wanted to say to her.

So much about today. About how dangerous, risky, and downright foolish it had been for her to follow him here.

About last night. How kissing her had awoken something in him that he'd thought was lost forever. How it terrified him, and shamed him, because it was stronger than anything he'd ever felt before. Ever.

And he had questions.

Questions like: how had she managed to get John to engage with her and actually act like a child for a brief time?

Why wasn't she crying and fainting about the horrors she'd travelled through to get here?

What was this hold she had over him?

Why couldn't he even imagine letting her go without a sharp, visceral pain shooting through his chest?

He opened his mouth, not even sure where to start.

And then, she smiled up at him.

And he didn't say a word.

He simply bent his head and kissed her.

Chapter Twenty-Two

ALISON HAD BEEN growing cold as the afternoon sun moved away from her wet skin, but the second Nic touched his lips to her own, she was in flames once more.

She hadn't been sure what to expect from him.

Anger, concern, disappointment?

When he'd merely stood and stared at her, she'd risked a smile, hoping to get one in return.

But, oh, this was so much better.

She dropped her boots and stockings and twined her arms around his neck, allowing herself to be swept away in the tide of feeling he had once again evoked in her.

Nic wrapped his arms around her and pulled her close. She pulled her mouth away, whilst she still had a tiny semblance of sense about her.

"My dress," she gasped. "Your clothes."

Nic pressed his lips to hers once more.

"I don't care about your dress," he growled against her mouth. "I don't care about my clothes."

His tongue delved inside her mouth, and she was

lost.

Desire, tumultuous and molten, crashed inside her, and she was caught in the maelstrom, unable and unwilling to escape.

She shuddered with need, desperate for something she couldn't name. Something only he could give her.

Suddenly, Nic pulled away from her.

"Christ, Alison," he croaked, pressing his brow against her own. "I'm sorry."

"Sorry?" She pulled back from him. "Why?"

He choked out a laugh.

"Because you're shivering with cold. Because I shouldn't keep manhandling you. Because I'm nowhere near as sorry as I should be."

"I am not shivering with cold," she argued, her need for him, her love for him loosening her tongue. "I am shivering from –"

She stopped herself just in time but felt her cheeks flush, and given the sudden unholy gleam in his eye, they gave her away.

He reached out a hand, grazing his knuckles along one cheek.

"Why you little wanton." He grinned.

Alison couldn't get enough of this playful, flirtatious side of Nic. Though he showed it but rarely, she knew it was there underneath the stern exterior.

"You're one to talk, your grace." She sniffed with faux haughtiness. "Yours is hardly the behaviour of a saint."

His smile became positively wolfish.

"Believe me, sweetheart. Around you, I feel like anything but a saint."

Her blood heated all over again at his words, and he suddenly stepped away from her, inhaling shakily.

"We need to get you inside and –" His eyes raked over her and he gulped. "And dry," he said hoarsely.

She looked down self-consciously, seeing the grass stains on her dress, the damp material clinging to her skin.

"Oh dear." She bit her lip. "I look a mess, don't I?"

"You look irresistible," he answered frankly. "Which is why we need to get you away from me and try to make you presentable for your brother-in-law."

It was Alison's turn to gulp.

Robert would definitely lock her in a tower when he saw her like this.

She nodded meekly and went to step around him.

He reached out and caught her arm, stopping her.

"And then," he said softly. "We are going to talk about how you came to be here, and what you were doing in St. Giles alone."

NIC PRESSED HIS fingers to his temples.

The girl was infuriating.

He sighed and dropped his hands to the desk in the small office he'd assigned himself when building the children's home.

"Alison," he said through gritted teeth, his jovial mood of earlier quite forgotten.

He'd sat and listened as best he could while she'd confessed that curiosity had sent her scurrying after him.

He must have aged a decade during her tale of hiring a bloody hack *by herself* and then stepping out alone into the streets outside his sanctuary.

She could have been killed. Genuinely killed.

"Do you have any idea of the danger you put yourself in?" he asked now, willing the images peppering his mind, tormenting him, to go away.

Images of the type of men outside these walls, more animal than human, and what they would do to a woman like Alison.

It made him sick just thinking of it.

She sighed and flipped her hair over her shoulder.

He really wished she wouldn't.

It was bad enough that he had to sit there keeping himself in check whilst it was flowing down her back like a waterfall of golden silk.

She'd been drying by the fire in his office, and he'd had to walk out and fetch a tray of tea like a damned maidservant to prevent himself from kissing her again.

Now, he was back.

She had her tea, her hair had dried into soft, golden curls around her face and down her back, and he was trying to talk some bloody sense into her.

"I already told you, Nicholas," she said, an edge of impatience to her voice now.

And damned if even that didn't cause a stirring of desire.

You're not a green lad, he told himself sternly. *Stop acting like one.*

"I didn't know quite what to expect. And I certainly shan't come alone next time. I'll take a maid, and –"

"What the hell do you mean, 'next time'?" he growled.

She blinked innocently, her eyes wide.

He didn't buy it for a second.

"Why next time I visit, of course. I've already told Bonnie I would come, and I should like to see John again, too. And I haven't even met the other children yet. I'm sure Mrs. Cafferty could find something for me to do to help."

He was speechless.

Could only stare at her as she chipped away at the wall of defence he had built, keeping her out.

She was absolutely sincere in what she was saying, he could tell.

She meant it. She was going to come back here. Here, where women of Quality didn't even like to *think* about, and spend time with these uneducated, unpolished children.

This wasn't supposed to happen.

She was supposed to be spoilt and frivolous, charming and untouched by the underbelly of the world around her.

Yet she would jump in fountains with motherless little girls, and coax volatile young boys into having some innocent fun.

She would come back here and not only spend time with these children willingly, but also seek out work to do for them.

In short, she was incredible, and unlike anyone he'd ever met.

But that was neither here nor there.

He would let her come back to this place over his dead body.

"Let me be very clear," he answered, enunciating every word so it got through that stubborn, lovely head of hers. "You will not be coming back here. Not with a maid. Not with an army."

Her eyes narrowed, and he sensed trouble.

"And who's going to stop me?" she asked, brow raised, light of challenge in her distracting eyes.

"Alison, it's not safe," he repeated. "You don't know these streets. This place. You don't know what can befall a young girl here."

"I know that you come here," she answered stubbornly. "I know that you help all of these people. Not just the children, but the people who work here. And I know that you have built hospitals and homes for people all around – oh, where was it?"

"Little Ireland," he answered woodenly, giving her the moniker of the slum, which housed thousands of Irish people who'd found themselves here for whatever unfortunate reason.

"Yes, Little Ireland. I thought it an odd name."

"So named because of the amount of Irish souls who find themselves there," he said wearily.

His grief, his guilt was starting to weigh heavily on his shoulders.

Never before had Nic felt the urge to talk about Ciara or his baby.

Yet with Alison happily chattering about being there, in that place, her goodness being sullied by the horrors to be found there, it was getting harder and harder to keep it inside.

"I suppose that's why it's so important to you?" she asked softly.

Nic's eyes snapped to Alison.

Surely, she didn't know.

She couldn't.

"I –" He wasn't sure what to say, but she didn't appear to be listening in any case.

"Abigail said your duchy is in Ireland. I should like to see Ireland." She smiled shyly, and his heart stopped dead in his chest.

His mind was whirling, his past and what he dearly wished could be his future merging so that he couldn't think straight.

Pinching the bridge of his nose, he climbed to his feet.

"Alison," he tried to drag the conversation and his emotions, back under his rigid control.

Why was it so damned difficult?

"You're not going near any of those places, or this place, again."

She frowned up at him.

"But I told Bonnie and John I would visit," she said. "And Lizzie mentioned that they don't have anyone to play for the children, so I thought that perhaps if there was a pianoforte, I could –"

"Damn it, I said no!" he yelled.

She looked shocked and hurt, and he felt like a monster.

"I could come with you."

God, but she was persistent.

"I wouldn't come to any harm with you. And –"

"Alison," he interrupted her, his exasperation clear in his voice. "I don't *want* you here. I don't want you in this place. I don't want you in the Rookery. I want you to say away."

She jumped to her feet.

"Why?" she demanded. "I want to help. I *would* have helped this whole time if I'd known about it."

Her statement sounded like an accusation.

Panic began to claw at him. Memories of Ciara. Of her body white and still. Of being told there had been no saving the babe.

"But you didn't tell me. You didn't tell anyone. Why on earth would you keep this wonderful part of your life from your friends? Why won't you let me in, Nic?"

"Because this is where the woman I was supposed to marry *died*," he shouted, finally, mercifully silencing her. "This is where I found out that my baby was dead. And I can't have you around it. I just can't."

He stormed out.

Like a coward, he strode out, leaving her with the poison of his words.

Chapter Twenty-Three

ALISON DIDN'T KNOW how long she stood there, the silence after Nic's departure deafening.

Her whole body felt frozen with shock.

He'd been engaged? He'd lost a child?

She shook her head in confusion.

Why would nobody tell her that? Not James, not Robert. Not even Abigail.

She ran over countless conversations in her head, trying to remember if anyone had ever mentioned anything about it.

Nic is a private person.

Nic doesn't share much about his life.

Nic keeps his cards close to his chest.

Robert said he came back a different person. One day he just…changed.

They didn't know!

Alison gasped aloud as the truth hit her.

Good lord. None of them knew!

And that meant this awful, horrible thing was a cross he bore alone.

Her breath hitched as she imagined the pain the proud, steady, dependable duke had been secretly carrying all these years.

Of their group of four, Nicholas was, she knew, the calm one. The one to whom they all turned.

He'd kept Robert from plunging into true madness in the years immediately following Gina's death.

He'd offered advice and a listening ear when Senna had turned James's world upside down with the news that his brother had been killed in cold blood.

And he'd always taken care of Simon, quietly and unassumingly. A voice of reason and a steady hand that stopped his friend from descending to depths of depravity from which there was no return.

But all the while, who was taking care of him?

Alison felt useless tears fill her eyes, and she impatiently blinked them away.

Tears were no good to him.

She sensed that he needed to talk about this.

Rushing out the door to try to find him, Alison ignored her own pain at his confession.

It was selfish of her to even think about it.

But the small, persistent voice couldn't be silenced.

All this time, she had thought Nic's honour and rigid control was keeping him from really letting her in, really opening himself up to her.

But in reality, he'd been grieving his lost love.

And though she was desperate to try to help him,

later on she would have to face the truth.

Nic was still in love with his deceased betrothed.

And Alison couldn't compete with a ghost.

AFTER HE'D LEFT Alison sitting in his office, he'd gone to hide himself away in the gardens. His emotions had been in chaos, his thoughts tumultuous. And Nic knew he wouldn't have been able to face anyone in that state. Wouldn't have wanted to. He never showed a lack of control to anyone, ever. Except Alison.

After a while, he'd come back in to seek out Mrs. Cafftery, hoping to find solace in discussing business and taking his mind well and truly off Alison Langton. But Mrs. Cafferty, like the rest of the home, was besotted with Miss Langton and couldn't sing her praises enough.

John had even joined the other children at dinner, Mrs. Cafferty had said, and told them all about playing in the fountain with the young Miss.

It was more than Nic could bear.

He'd told Alison something that he'd sworn to himself he would take to the grave.

Then he'd run from her.

Now, he had to sit and listen to how wonderful she was, as though he didn't already know.

He'd called for his carriage and asked Mrs. Cafferty

to send for Alison.

And then he'd waited outside for her. And waited. And waited.

He knew she approached because he'd been attuned to her for so long now, without even realising it, that he knew when she was near.

His heart knew. His very soul knew.

Nic took a fortifying breath and turned to face her.

She was pale and drawn.

And that was his fault.

Without a word, he offered a hand to help her, ignoring the *fission* of awareness that even now skittered along his nerves.

"I'm sorry I took so long," she muttered when Nic had taken the seat across from her and closed the carriage door, banging on the ceiling to instruct the driver to move. "But I didn't want to leave without saying goodbye to John and Bonnie. And then there were the rest of the children to meet."

"It's fine," he mumbled, hating himself for creating this void between them.

Had it really only been weeks since he'd thought her a spoilt, selfish brat?

How she had changed him, completely and irrevocably, in such a short space of time.

The silence between them grew oppressive.

And for the first time in ten years, Nic had no idea what to do. He felt lost and helpless. A feeling he didn't like. A feeling he'd fought hard to overcome for most of his adult life.

In the end, he wasn't the one to break it.

"What happened, Nic?"

He had a choice to make.

He could do what he'd always done and keep that part of his life locked away. Free from pity and prying eyes. He could preserve the memory of Ciara and the idea of his babe without the ugliness of what had happened encroaching on it.

Or he could, for once in his life, allow someone in. Share the burden of his grief and sacrifice some of the rigidity of his control over his emotions.

He gazed across the carriage at the beautiful woman who had snuck into his heart without him even noticing.

He didn't want to sully her with the ugly realities of the lives around here.

But it was temping; the idea of letting someone else share the load he carried.

Suddenly, Alison leaned forward and gripped his hand in her own tiny one.

"You're so strong for everyone else, Nic." She looked up at him, her eyes glistening. "But you cannot keep all of your own troubles hidden away. The people who care about you, who – who love you –" His heart stuttered at the word. "They would want to know. To understand."

He shook his head.

"There's no point. It was a long time ago," he muttered.

"Yes, and it has affected you every day since, I'll warrant," she persisted. "It's why you take care of everyone. Why you put so much effort into helping the people here."

She was right. There was no point in denying it.

"But you're allowed to be vulnerable, Nic," she said, squeezing his hand. "You're allowed to grieve and take strength from others. Take strength from me."

"I don't want you hearing this," he said stubbornly. "I never wanted you around all of this."

"Well, that's too bad," she said, sitting back and dropping his hand. And damned if he didn't want to snatch it right back. "Because I know about the children now, and I've promised to come back and play for them. And –" She raised her voice when he opened his mouth to object. "Mrs. Cafferty has promised to show me the women's home and the hospitals you've built."

"Alison –"

"I want to do this, Nic," she interrupted softly. "But I can promise not to do it without you. If you really don't want me here, then I won't come back. But I'm asking you to let me be a part of it. I'll never come without you. And I know I'll not be in any danger when I'm with you."

Oh God.

Her words were like a dagger to the heart.

She was so trusting. So willing to put her safety in his hands so she could come here and give of herself to people less fortunate.

But how could he be sure he'd be able to protect her when he couldn't protect Ciara and his unborn child?

He didn't deserve Alison's trust.

"I won't make you take me back here," she reiterated, unaware of the maelstrom of emotions he was caught in. "And I won't make you tell me about your past. But I want you to let me in. The decision is yours."

They faced each other across the carriage, only inches separating them, yet it felt like so much more.

He knew then that he was going to tell her, just as he knew he was going to bring her back here as often as she wanted.

Because, whether he was willing to admit it to her or not, Nic was never going to be able to tell her no.

Chapter Twenty-Four

NICHOLAS RACED THROUGH the streets of London, ignoring shouts of protest as his stallion pounded the ground, dodging carriages and people as he went.

It wasn't safe to ride at breakneck speed, of course, but he was beyond caring.

He'd found her!

After months of searching, he'd found her.

His child would be born by now. He didn't even know if it was a son or daughter, and he didn't care.

All that mattered was his sleepless nights, the money spent, the trips up and down the length and breadth of Ireland and England had finally produced results.

When word had arrived in a short note from his investigator that a young girl confirmed to be Ciara Connelly had been found in The Rookery, Nic hadn't even bade his friends farewell.

He simply got up from the table at James's town-house and bolted.

The entire time that he rode toward St. Giles, he thought about what he would say.

How could he even begin to apologise for what had happened?

Would Ciara believe him when he explained that he had done everything in his power to find her and their baby?

He arrived at the address given, and his stomach roiled, not just because of the stench and filth everywhere, but because of the guilt he felt that the girl he'd promised to take care of had ended up here.

Had his baby really been born in such a place? The grandchild of the Duke of Barnbury?

His guilt was like a live thing, slithering inside him, poisoning his very blood, consuming him.

Dismounting Apollo, he called to a nearby urchin, handing over a bag of coin, promising plenty more if he took good care of the horse.

Then, taking a deep breath, he hammered on the cracked, peeling wood of the door.

Nic's heart sputtered erratically as he waited for someone to open the door.

When it finally creaked, he looked into the eyes of a stern-looking, stout woman.

"Can I help you?" she asked, keeping the flimsy door between them, her Irish brogue distinctive, reminding him of home.

A home he'd left behind and would never return to.

As though that would keep him out.

"I am Nicholas Fyfe," he said, trying to keep the impatience from his voice.

He knew St. Giles was unsafe. And he didn't want to risk anything happening to him before he could rescue Ciara and his child.

"I was told that Ciara Connelly was here."

The woman ran a suspicious eye over him.

"Please," he said again, sensing that she wouldn't allow him entry. "She was sent away by my father, the Duke of Barnbury. I've been trying to find her. Find them both."

The woman's faded green eyes snapped back to his face, and Nic thought he detected a hint of pity in their depths.

"I'm Mrs. Cafferty, my lord," the woman said before stepping back and making room for him to step inside the hovel. "I think you should come in."

Nic's trepidation increased tenfold as he stepped inside.

What he saw shocked him to his core.

He had heard about the conditions around this part of London. But to witness it with his own eyes was something else entirely.

He was in a room. Just one room, with gaping holes in the ceiling and buckets of slop dotted around the place.

Everywhere he looked there were curtains and sheets

hung haphazardly.

"What –?" he began to ask, but as his eyes adjusted to the gloom, he saw that there were people behind each curtain, children darting in and out of them.

"What is this place?" he asked Mrs. Cafferty, unable to stomach what he was seeing.

"It's where we live, my lord," the lady answered matter-of-factly.

"The curtains?"

"Privacy for the families, my lord."

Good God.

Nic ran a horror-filled gaze around the room once more.

Families? The entire place was smaller than a potting shed on his family's lands.

"Where is she?" he asked, all at once desperate to remove Ciara and their child from this place.

Mrs. Cafferty sighed as though the weight of the world were on her shoulders.

"You're a good man, my lord," she said. "I can sense it. You have honour and a kind heart."

"Thank you," he answered, humbled if a little confused.

"That's why it saddens me to tell you this."

Nic's breath froze in his chest.

"Go on," he said stoically. Bracing himself for the blow.

Mrs. Cafferty shook her head sadly.

"The girls that come to me when they're in trouble, they never have the man that did it come looking for them," she said forthrightly. "And they're never in a good way when I get them."

"I do my best, my lord," she continued sadly. "But it's not often good enough. And it wasn't this time."

She took a deep breath, then looked him square in the eye.

"I'm sorry, my lord," she repeated. "But Ciara was badly beaten when she arrived here, and she was about to give birth to your son. It was far too early. She hasn't recovered, and she's not going to. We're just waiting for it now."

He couldn't move. Couldn't breathe.

A son.

"And the babe," Mrs Cafferty continued, with Nic having to force himself not to cover his ears, to refuse to hear what was coming. "He didn't survive."

ALISON DIDN'T SPEAK, and he was glad of it.

Unburdening himself for the first time meant reliving it all over again, and the grief felt as fresh as if he'd been told yesterday.

Even all these years later, he didn't allow Mrs. Cafferty to speak of it to him.

"I went in to see Ciara," he said, his tone emotionless, refusing to look at her. "She was delirious with fever. She didn't even know I was there. The next day, Mrs. Cafferty sent word that she was gone."

The news had sent Nic's despair spiralling.

Just another knife to the gut.

He had cried and howled to the heavens at the injustice of it all.

But there was no escaping his grief and his guilt.

And so, he'd done what was necessary to survive.

He took everything he was feeling in an iron grip, and he buried it.

Over the years, he had forgiven himself. Or at least learned to live with it.

Unlike Robert's guilt that had clawed at him every waking and sleeping moment, Nic's was like a dull ache, always in the background but never consuming him. Because he simply didn't allow it to.

A week after they'd buried Ciara, unable to do so for his son since Mrs. Cafferty didn't know where he'd been taken by the midwife who'd assisted in his birth, he'd told Mrs. Cafferty that he didn't want anyone else ending up like Ciara if he could help it.

Of course, he couldn't save them all.

Nobody could.

The world was what it was, and Nic was fighting an uphill battle. But he'd never stop.

Mrs. Cafferty had been more than a helping hand in setting up his various homes and hospitals.

She'd been a mother of sorts. Close, but never too close.

Alison still didn't speak, and Nic prepared himself for her horror. Her revulsion. Even her judgment.

Finally, he couldn't stand the wait any longer, and he looked over at her.

She was sitting quietly, tears running unchecked down her face, and those tears nearly brought him to his knees.

He couldn't stand it.

Couldn't stand to see her cry.

"Alison." His voice sounded broken to his own ears.

It was just a word. Just her name.

But it set her in motion, and she suddenly flew across the carriage, into his lap, and buried her head in his shoulder.

"I'm sorry, Nic," she sniffled, her voice thick with tears, her delicate hands twining around his neck. "I'm so, so sorry."

Chapter Twenty-Five

ALISON WAS HALF expecting Nic to push her away, especially when he stiffened.

But after a second, his shoulders sagged, and he wrapped her in his arms.

"Shh," he whispered into her hair, kissing the top of her head, offering *her* comfort when it was *he* who'd had such unspeakable tragedy in his life. "It's all right," he soothed. "Please, don't cry."

And of course, that made her cry harder, for even now he was still taking care of other people.

"Alison, please." She heard real distress in his voice. "I can't bear to see you cry."

She lifted her head and wiped her eyes, determined to be strong for him.

He lifted a hand, his thumb capturing a stray tear.

"All the work you do," she said tremulously.

He shrugged with a nonchalance he couldn't possibly feel.

"I couldn't help Ciara or my son." He swallowed hard. "But I can do my best to help others."

"You did everything you could for Ciara and your

son," Alison insisted, reaching up and cupping his face when he would have looked away.

He needed to hear this.

"Nic, what happened to them was awful. Just awful. But there was *nothing* more you could have done. You can't punish yourself over it. You can't carry it alone. Please, don't do that to yourself."

He stared at her, his navy-blue eyes unreadable, and she couldn't even begin to imagine what was going through his head.

Finally, he smiled a small smile.

"I'm not carrying it alone," he said softly. "Not anymore."

Alison's heart thudded painfully at his words.

She was emotionally drained from their talk, from the whole day.

So, she could only imagine how he felt.

"You've never told any of them." It was a statement, not a question.

Nic sighed, shaking his head slightly.

"I couldn't," he finally said. "I was only able to live with what happened by burying it. Trying to make amends through my charitable work and living my life as though it hadn't happened to me."

"They would have helped," she said, knowing it was true.

Robert, James, and Simon would do anything for Nicholas, just like he would do anything for them.

"I didn't know how to let them," he confessed. "I was certain nobody could."

He gazed into her eyes until she forgot to breathe, and she only took a gulp of air when she became lightheaded.

"Now, I'm not so sure," he said.

Oh Lord.

Her heart would never survive him saying such things.

Alison was appalled to feel desire stir to life inside her.

This was not the time!

He'd just been telling her about the loss of the love of his life, and of his poor, innocent baby.

And what had she done? Thrown herself at him, that's what.

And worse, now she wanted quite desperately to kiss him.

She was shameless. A hussy.

She pushed against his chest, trying to free herself from his arms.

To her surprise, he tightened his grip.

"Where are you going?" he demanded.

Alison's laugh was a little breathless.

"I was returning to my side," she said. "I thought I should –"

"You should stay right where you are," he insisted, and her heart burst with happiness, foolish though that was.

"Thank you for telling me," she said quietly.

He reached up and tucked a lock of hair behind her ear.

"Thank you for wanting to know," he said. "You're the only person who's ever secretly followed me to find out the truth about me."

He frowned as though remembering how unhappy he was about that, and she smiled sheepishly at him.

"I meant what I said, Alison," his tone brooked no argument. "I don't want you going back there."

She opened her mouth to object, but before she could, he spoke again.

"At least never alone," he continued, and she tried not to feel smug that he was giving in on this. "And not with anyone but me."

"I won't go back with anyone else," she told him sincerely. "Only you."

ONLY YOU.

That's all she'd said.

Only you.

Nic's mind was whirring, his heart thumping.

Those two simple words were enough to bring the rest of the wall around his heart tumbling down.

And in the dust, the truth he'd hidden from, shied

away from, was suddenly, startlingly clear. He'd known for weeks, of course, deep down he'd known, but now he didn't have the strength to deny it any longer.

Somehow, Nic had done what he'd believed impossible.

He'd fallen helplessly, hopelessly in love.

This slip of a girl with her impish smile, her mischievous disregard for rules, and heart-breaking blue eyes had revived his long dead heart then taken it for her own.

She sighed contentedly and burrowed further into his chest, her head resting against his heart, where she belonged.

He knew it, without quite knowing how.

She was exactly where she should be, always. In his arms. Right next to his heart.

He should have known when he opened up to her in a way he had never done with a single soul before.

Should have known when her tears caused him more visceral pain than he'd felt in years.

He wanted her so much that he ached for her.

But it went further than that.

He needed her, too. Needed her to bring lightness to his life. To remind him to *live* and not just exist to fulfill a duty that would never end.

He needed her to laugh with him and eat ices with him. To dance with him and make fun of his seriousness every once in a while.

Bending his head, Nic placed a gentle kiss on the top of her head, intoxicated by the floral scent of her.

He felt drained and ragged from the emotional turmoil of the afternoon.

His body felt exhausted yet exhilarated.

How could he feel so desperately sad for Ciara, for his son, yet so happy and content at merely having Alison in his arms?

How could he feel like weeping for his past and be anxious to start a new future?

And, he felt a fresh twinge of guilt, how could he be remembering Ciara and the promises he'd made to her, all the while realising that he'd never loved her the way he loved the woman he was holding?

His love for Ciara had been real, Nic was sure of it.

But he had loved her with a boy's heart, he realised now. A boy whose heart had been untouched by sorrow.

Now he was a man. A man who had experienced grief and loss.

He was damaged. More damaged than he'd realised before Alison had forced him to confront his past.

But with the sorrow came a new depth of feeling, a greater capacity to love.

And the love he had for Alison was all-consuming, deep, unstoppable, and eternal.

And terrifying because of it.

Things had become very complicated, very quickly.

Nic ran a hand up and down Alison's back, relishing the fact that he was touching her like this, holding her like this.

But he couldn't fully enjoy the moment.

He'd kissed her, fallen in love with her, shared his work with her, his past with her.

Yet, what did it matter if he loved her? If he took solace just from holding her? What did it matter that he only felt truly alive now when he was around her, now when he realised he hadn't really been living before her?

Did that change anything?

For so many years, he hadn't considered himself to be someone who could share his life with a woman.

He knew that most *ton* marriages existed only for the merging of powerful names, of linking wealth and status, and for Peers especially, to do their duty and carry on the family name.

But he'd never be able to do that with Alison. He'd never be able to live a separate life from her.

Already, he missed her too much when she wasn't around.

If she belonged to him, if she were his, he'd never be able to drag himself away from her.

But the only way he'd been able to live with himself for these past ten years was by dedicating his entire life to helping people like Ciara, children like his son might have been if he'd lived.

Was he really going to turn his back on all of that?

Alison had been silent throughout his musings, and he found himself quite desperate to know what she was thinking.

Yet far too much had happened tonight for him to have that particular conversation.

He simply wasn't ready.

The carriage rolled to a stop, and Nic saw they were outside Robert's townhouse.

"Sweetheart," the endearment slipped out without conscious thought. "We're home."

He was surprised by the aching need that little sentenced evoked in him.

A part of him, a strong, undeniable part, wished that she were his and they would have a lifetime of nights like this, where she'd rest in his arms and he'd awaken her outside the home they shared together.

She sat up and smiled shyly at him and though he hadn't even begun to unravel the complicated tangle of his thoughts, he couldn't help but lean forward and press his lips softly to hers.

He purposely held back, refusing to unleash any of the passion that always lurked below the surface.

He placed her gently on the bench across from him so he could open the carriage door and get her inside.

But no sooner had he let go of her than the door swung open and Robert's furious face glared at the pair of them.

"You," he rounded on Alison, whose eyes popped open at his tone. "Where the hell have you been?"

Chapter Twenty-Six

A LISON HAD BEEN exhausted, worn out from the day's events, but Robert's tone quickly woke her up.

She'd never seen him this angry.

Never heard him speak to anyone like that, certainly not her.

She had a feeling she was getting a glimpse of the bad-tempered monster he used to be.

"I–I–" She didn't know where to start but as it turned out, she didn't need to.

"Don't speak to her like that."

Her eyes snapped to Nic, and her stomach plummeted at the look of anger between the two men.

It reminded her of that night at the theatre that seemed a lifetime ago. Only the roles were reversed now, and it was Robert who was furiously angry, and Nicholas jumping to her defence.

She watched with sick apprehension as the gentlemen engaged in yet another silent battle of wills.

Finally, to her relief, Robert's expression cleared somewhat.

"Your sister was worried," he said to Alison, his tone flat, his eyes coloured slate with contained anger. "We came back, and you were gone with no explanation. The servants said you ran out of the house."

"I'm sorry." She gulped. And she was. Truly. "I–I forgot that – um…"

"She obviously forgot to tell you that I asked her to accompany me to one of my charitable homes this afternoon," Nic said smoothly, so calmly, that even Alison nearly believed it.

"One of your what?" Robert frowned in obvious confusion, and Alison took advantage of the moment to jump from the carriage and hurry by him.

She didn't hear if Nic even responded.

As she dashed up the steps to the front door, she did hear Robert enquire stiffly as to whether Nicholas was staying to dine with them.

Worried that he'd refuse, Alison turned to implore him.

"Please, stay," she said quietly.

He looked at Alison, and Robert looked at him.

"I'll stay," he said, and she beamed at him before rushing inside to change out of her ruined gown, lest Robert really lose his temper.

She and Nic had so much to talk about, Alison knew.

He had loved deeply and suffered the most unimaginable loss.

But he'd also shared that with her, let her see a glimpse of the life he kept hidden from the world.

Ciara must have been special to have captured a heart like Nic's.

Alison felt a pang of sadness.

Nicholas hadn't recovered from the death of Ciara and his son because he hadn't properly grieved for them. Shutting himself off emotionally wasn't healing.

She was determined to help him.

She loved him too much to let him continue to live that way.

And if it hurt like a dagger to the heart to help the man she loved mourn the loss of the woman *he* had loved, then that was the price she would have to pay.

NICHOLAS WATCHED HER go, aware that Robert's eyes were boring into him.

Muttering an oath under his breath, he turned to face one of his oldest friends.

"I know," he said before Robert could even speak.

"Good," was the quick, sharp response.

Then with a sigh, Robert slapped him on the back before leading the way inside.

Stepping into the drawing room, Nicholas took in Abigail's speculative look, Senna's slight smile, and James's frown that could give Robert's a run for its

238

money.

Marvellous.

It was odd for Nic to be on the receiving end of any sort of censure. Usually, it was the other way around.

The only thing that would make this worse would be if –

"We're the last to arrive, then."

If Simon came.

Nic turned to see Simon run his black gaze speculatively over the room, Amelia eyeing them curiously by his side.

The tension was palpable, and Simon would recognise it, since in the past he had caused that atmosphere almost everywhere he went.

He frowned slightly then held up his hands.

"I can't have done anything this time," he said. "I'm barely back in the country."

Before anyone could answer him, Alison swept into the room looking beautiful and perfectly put together in mint-green silk, her hair piled atop her head.

Nobody would ever guess she'd been dancing barefoot in fountains only hours ago.

Without thinking, Nic stepped forward to greet her.

There was an immediate cessation in the chatter around the room.

"Ah, so it's not me," Simon laughed.

"Shh," Amelia scolded.

The bell rang for dinner, and the group awkwardly shuffled toward the dining room.

"I told you," Simon said in a whisper loud enough to be heard in France. "Didn't I tell you?"

"Yes, darling," Amelia responded with practised patience. "Now, shh."

Nic had been grateful to the ladies at dinner when they'd kept the conversation light and easy.

He couldn't help but feel this evening had been some sort of trap.

Why else would both James and Simon have just happened to come along at dinner time?

He'd been grateful again to the ladies when they'd insisted on shirking convention by having the gentlemen join them in the drawing room straight after dinner, foregoing their usual port and cheroots.

Much as it irritated him, though, to think he'd been brought here to be interrogated, he had to admit how nice it was.

If he were willing to give less of his time to St. Giles and come back into Society in a real way, attending events and taking more interest in his various estates and holdings, if he were to marry Alison and no longer keep himself so far removed from everyone, even his friends, there'd be countless dinners like this one.

Perhaps without the tension that still crackled around the room.

This evening was like so many they'd shared before.

They talked, they laughed.

But Nic felt strangely removed from it all.

He ran his gaze around the room.

Amelia had her nose buried in a book, pointing things out to Simon, who pretended to look but watched her instead, playing with tendrils of her hair.

James and Senna stood by the window, James whispering in her ear before kissing her softly, his hand resting on her swelling belly.

Robert and Abigail were as they ever where, not speaking much but enclosed in a bubble that surrounded just the two of them, their love obvious from just the way they looked at each other.

And that's when Nic realised why he felt so distant tonight, so removed.

His eyes inevitably moved to her.

Alison sat at the pianoforte playing softly, her eyes on the keys.

It was because none of this felt like his life anymore.

Being here with his friends, being the only one of them single, it never would have bothered him before. Not in the slightest.

But now it didn't seem right that he wasn't with

Alison, sitting beside her on the piano bench, listening to her play, watching her fingers spring lightly over the keys.

His whole life should be with her, by her side.

Just as all his friends, unusual though it was in the *ton,* were blatant in their admiration and affections for their wives, so, too, should Nic be with Alison.

But he couldn't.

Much as he had to use all his willpower not to go to her, he simply couldn't.

They hadn't spoken of a future because Nic didn't know if they had one.

He hadn't told her he loved her because he'd been too cowardly to admit it even to himself until today.

He loved her so much that he ached for her.

But he couldn't go to her.

"I don't think you've blinked for ten minutes straight."

Simon's voice by his side distracted Nic, and he turned to see his friend offer a tumbler of brandy.

He hadn't even noticed his friend move, that's how wrapped up in Alison he'd been.

He mumbled his thanks, took the tumbler, and swallowed the contents in a single gulp.

Simon raised a brow but didn't comment on the unusual action.

Nic conducted his drinking moderately and sensibly as he did with everything in his life.

x

Everything but Alison.

His gaze was drawn to her again, and he saw that she'd now joined Amelia on the chaise, the two of them chattering happily.

"Nic."

Simon's voice was low and serious.

He turned to see his friend watching him closely.

"What's going on?"

"I don't know," he mumbled miserably.

He didn't even have the energy to present his usual stoic demeanour.

Simon reached out and gripped his shoulder briefly.

"You'd better figure it out quickly," he warned gently. "Because both James and Robert are going to want an answer."

Chapter Twenty-Seven

T HE ONLY SOUND in the room was the ticking of the longcase clock in the corner.

Nic didn't want to break said silence and didn't know how, in any case.

Abigail and Alison had retired hours ago.

He hadn't managed anything more than a formal bow to her, not with the eyes of her guardians boring into him.

Senna and Amelia had left soon after, leaving James and Simon behind.

Now the four of them sat in Rob's study, facing each other and not saying a word.

"I must say," Simon suddenly piped up. "It feels strange to be on the other side of this. Usually, I'm the one in trouble. It's quite a novelty – getting to sit here and judge someone else. Rather enjoyable."

Nic scowled at him, earning an unrepentant grin.

"But," Simon continued. "If someone wouldn't mind catching me up?"

"Only Nic can do that."

Nic turned at Rob's quietly spoken words.

"Would you like to explain why Alison ran out of here this morning and then ended up coming back with you, looking like she'd been dragged through a hedge?"

Ah, he'd noticed that.

"I told you, she must have forgotten –"

"Nic."

He stopped at James's interruption, turning to look into eyes the exact colour of Alison's.

"You've never lied to us before, please, don't start now."

Nic almost laughed aloud.

Never lied to them before? Perhaps, technically that was true. But he'd kept them from his life, his real life, for the past ten years.

"What is it you want me to say?"

"Robert seems to think that there might be something between you and Alison."

"Actually, I *know* there's something between you and Alison," Robert interrupted. "Just like I know something happened the other night at Vauxhall."

"Wait, what?" James snapped. "You never told me that."

He turned to glare at Nicholas, who felt a sudden tightening of his cravat.

"Vauxhall Gardens?" Simon, who was decidedly *not* helping. "Why, I didn't think you had it in you, Saint Nic."

NADINE MILLARD

"There's nothing bloody saintly about him," Robert glowered.

"And little Alison Langton. I thought I detected a little devilment in her. Though a secret assignation in the Gardens with this paragon of virtue is something of a surprise."

"Shut up, Simon," Nic finally snapped.

He hated hearing Simon speak of Alison that way. Though from the glares the laughing earl was receiving from James and Robert, he wasn't the only one feeling that way.

"Nothing happened in the Gardens," Nic lied. "And nothing happened today."

That felt like an even bigger lie.

So much had happened today. But that was between him and Alison.

And until he had the chance to speak to her, he certainly wasn't going to discuss anything with her cousin and brother-in-law.

And Simon, apparently.

"Why are you even here?" he rounded on Simon. "This doesn't concern you."

"Oh, I know that," Simon said with his usual devilish smirk. "I'm just here for the show."

Nic simply rolled his eyes then turned back to Robert and James.

"You've known me for almost my whole life," he said. "You know that I would never take advantage of an innocent miss. Especially not Abigail's sister, for God's sake."

Robert and James shared a glance then, to Nic's relief, nodded simultaneously.

"That's why I was so shocked," Rob said. "It's not like you, Nic. Usually you know better. But with Ally –"

He shrugged.

"You're different. I see it. James sees it. Even Abigail sees it."

"Yet you disliked her so." James took up the thread of the conversation. "Didn't you think her quite spoilt?"

"A spoilt, selfish, brat, if memory serves."

"Simon." Nic turned to the interfering devil. "I told you to shut up."

"But you did say it," he persisted like a stubborn bloody child.

"Yes, I said it." Nic was exasperated now. He wanted to get home.

He needed to think. To process everything that had happened today.

He needed to see Alison.

But before all that, he needed to appease his best friends.

"Nic, you are the most decent, trustworthy person I know, aside from James," Robert said, ignoring Simon's "ahem." "If you tell me there's nothing between you and Alison, then I'll believe you."

"You must know we would never have an objection to you," James said.

"Um, you warned me away from both of your cousins under pain of death," Simon said to James. "And Senna, if I recall."

James raised a brow at Simon. "That's hardly the same."

Simon glared at James for a moment before shrugging.

"Fair enough," he said. "As you were."

Nic looked at his three closest friends, more brothers really, all gazing back at him.

He didn't want to lie to them.

But didn't Alison deserve to hear how he felt before anyone else?

He determined he wouldn't outright deny it, but he wouldn't confess the truth either.

Slipping on his mask of stoicism, the one he'd worn for ten years, Nic looked Robert and James in the eye.

"I warned you a year ago that you had trouble on your hands with her," he said, feeling like the worst sort of cad. "It cannot be a surprise to you that her behaviour has been a little unorthodox."

"It's a surprise that you're involved, Nic," Rob interjected.

Well, he had him there.

"What exactly are your intentions?" James asked.

Nic would dearly love to know the answer to that

question himself.

He knew what he wanted. Knew how desperately he wished to spend every single day for the rest of his life with Alison.

But he didn't yet know how to walk away from his work in St. Giles and all the people who relied on him there.

And he sure as hell didn't want Alison anywhere near there if he could help it.

He would take her back because he'd promised to and he didn't trust her to stay away. But he didn't want her sullied by the realities of life in the underbelly of London.

James and Robert stared at him, making him feel like a criminal in the docks.

Even Simon had stopped joking around.

Nic needed to give them an answer.

But he hadn't even given himself one.

"I don't have any," he said because he didn't know *what* his intentions were right then.

Robert sighed and moved to refill all their glasses.

"I didn't think we'd ever be here, Nic," he said as he handed over a tumbler of brandy. "Not with you."

Nic merely looked at him, refusing to drop his gaze.

"I would never pressure you to do something you don't want to do," Robert said finally. "But this cannot continue. You might not love Ally, but according to

Abby, she's becoming infatuated with you."

Nic's heart thumped painfully at Robert's words.

He wanted to argue, tell his friend that, of course, he loved Ally. He could barely breathe with the strength of his feelings for her.

"You need to stay away from her," James said bluntly, but not unkindly. "The time alone together – if you were anyone else, we couldn't have allowed it to begin with. Now, with the risk of Alison being hurt, it ends."

The lance of pain that ran through Nic at James's words was all the proof he needed that he couldn't ever let her go.

But that didn't change the fact that he needed time to rearrange his life. He needed to find a way to step away from St. Giles without feeling like a monster for doing so. And he needed to reconnect with the life he'd left behind ten years ago.

Only then would he ask Alison to become his duchess. His wife.

ALISON LEANED HER head against the closed study door, squeezing her eyes shut to stop any tears from slipping past.

She'd only come down here to make sure she wasn't the cause of any discord between the gentlemen.

And apparently, she wasn't.

They weren't angry with Nicholas.

They weren't going to try to force his hand.

No, instead they wanted to tell him to leave her alone.

To tell him that she was smitten with him, as though she were a schoolgirl incapable of any real depth of feeling.

Her heart had stopped dead in her chest as she'd willed Nicholas to admit to caring about her, if not loving her.

Their afternoon together, his opening up to her, their earth-shattering kisses – they had to mean *something*, didn't they?

Yet, he'd said it meant nothing.

And now they all sat in there, feeling sorry for her, pitying her for her infatuation while he thought her a spoilt, selfish, brat.

Those had been his words.

I don't have any.

That's what he'd said when Robert had questioned him about his intentions.

Alison felt like a prized idiot.

All this evening, though she couldn't go to him, she'd carried the memory of their afternoon inside her like a delicious secret.

She'd allowed herself to fantasize about one day being his wife.

They would spend their days in London, even in the winter months. They would work together at the homes and hospitals Nic had dedicated his life to.

They would work side by side doing their best to save as many people as possible from the tragic fate of Ciara and her baby.

Of course, Nic had never said he loved her or wanted to marry her. And she knew he still loved his lost betrothed.

But she had hoped that he had at least come to care for her. She had enough love for both of them.

And perhaps one day, he might even grow to love her, too.

But standing outside Robert's door now, listening to their discussion move on to other things, Alison realised she'd been fooling herself.

Perhaps he didn't think she was quite so spoilt now. But that meant nothing.

James had told him he'd have to end their friendship, and Nicholas had said nothing.

She'd had questions about them, about a future between them, about how he felt about her.

And now she had her answer.

His silence spoke volumes.

Alison turned slowly and walked away.

Chapter Twenty-Eight

NIC FROWNED AS he ran his eyes over the ballroom, barely hearing his name being announced.

The Season was moving along, and it wouldn't be long before London began to empty again.

This year, for the first time, he'd be leaving with them.

It was time.

He was going home.

Back to Ireland.

And if he had his way, he'd be taking Alison with him as his wife.

Nic knew now that he should have just told Robert, James, and Simon last night what he intended.

Because one way or another, he wanted to have Alison by his side, as his wife. No matter what it took to sort through all the other stuff, that was non-negotiable. He couldn't live without her. And he didn't want to try.

He'd spoken to Mrs. Cafferty at length that morning about his guilt over thinking about leaving his work in the hands of others, about falling in love with

Alison, about thinking about becoming a father when he'd never allowed himself to imagine such a thing.

Of course, the formidable Irishwoman had been blunt in her opinion. She'd told him he was foolish to have waited this long to tell Alison how he felt when it was clear as day to anyone who was around them.

She'd told him that he'd done more for the people of St. Giles, and Little Ireland in particular, in ten years than most people did in their lifetimes, and nobody would ever begrudge him the chance at happiness.

It had felt like a validation he hadn't known he'd been searching for.

And with her words came a realisation; Nic needed to start being honest with his friends, and with himself.

He had more responsibilities than he'd been willing to deal with these past years. He had a duty to more than the residents of St. Giles.

Though he kept abreast of all his holdings through communications with his excellent stewards and men of business, it wasn't the same.

He needed to tell Alison how he felt and ask her to marry him.

He needed to tell his friends of his past.

And he needed to go home.

But before all that, he needed to find her.

He spotted Simon and Amelia and made his way toward them, smiling and nodding at various greetings, ignoring more than one set of lashes batting at him.

As he got closer to the couple, he saw that they were frowning, their heads bent together, whispering furiously.

Nic didn't particularly want to encroach on what seemed a rather serious conversation, but then he heard Alison's name and without thought, he spoke up.

"What's going on?" he asked without preamble.

Simon and Amelia looked at him, matching looks of concern on their faces.

"Um, well – "Amelia seemed to be hedging her words.

"Alison's gone rogue," Simon blurted.

Nic frowned in confusion.

"What? What do you mean?"

Simon sighed.

"I mean –" He turned and nodded his head toward the other side of the packed ballroom. "The devilment in her I spoke about last night seems to have come out in force this evening."

Nic whipped his head in the direction Simon was nodding and a black fury, sudden and swift, coursed through him.

Alison looked as heart-wrenchingly beautiful as ever he'd seen her, and his body reacted immediately, even as his mind worked furiously to understand what he was seeing.

She was in an ice-blue, satin gown, her hair up,

showing off her slender neck.

She looked as perfect and beautiful as she ever did. That was not unusual.

The fact that she was surrounded by some of the worst scoundrels in the *ton,* laughing and tapping them lightly with her fan, resting a hand on the arm of that bastard Fulham and whispering in his ear? That was most definitely unusual.

"What the hell is going on?" Nic bit out, finding it harder than ever to keep up the façade of indifference with the prying eyes of the *ton* all around them.

"I don't know," Amelia whispered.

She glanced around, and Nic followed her lead, seeing to his dismay that Alison was gaining the attention of more than one loose-lipped gossip.

"Where's Robert? Or James?"

Amelia sighed, pushing her spectacles up her nose.

"Robert and Abigail stayed at home with Lottie this evening," she explained quickly. "James and Senna have yet to arrive. I told Alison we'd be happy to take her with us this evening, of course. But as soon as we arrived, she was like a woman possessed!"

"She drank more champagne in the first half an hour of being here than I've ever seen her consume," Simon added helpfully.

"And you didn't stop her?" Nic scowled.

"That's what you've caught us arguing about," Simon answered flatly. "Amelia seems to think if I go over there and remove Fulham's arms for him, it might create something of a scene."

"So, we just leave her over there with him?"

"Of course, not," Amelia responded. "But her reputation won't withstand either of you going over there and making a spectacle of yourselves," she said firmly. "Now, if we can just –"

Simon's black oath interrupted whatever she'd been about to say, and Nic and Amelia turned to see what he was swearing at.

Lord Severill had just joined Alison's little party by the balcony doors.

Lord Severill, who had attacked Amelia at Simon's house party last year. And who Simon had nearly killed with his bare hands as a result.

"I'd say this calls for a spectacle, love," Simon said. "Wouldn't you agree, Nic?"

But Nicholas didn't answer.

He was already halfway across the room.

ALISON SMILED HER thanks as someone pressed another glass of champagne into her hand.

She couldn't exactly say that she was having a good time, but at least the cacophony of chatter and laughter around her was a good distraction from her heartache.

Earlier that day when Abigail had said they were

going to have a quiet evening at home as Lottie was a little under the weather, Alison's stomach had dropped.

She had cried herself to a fitful sleep the night before, waking at dawn only to cry all over again.

And she couldn't face another night of that.

Thankfully, when Amelia had called, she'd happily offered to have Alison join her at tonight's soiree.

Alison had taken care with her preparations, choosing one of her nicest gowns and allowing Eliza to spend an age threading a ribbon of blue silk intricately through her curls.

As soon as she'd arrived in the ballroom, she had looked for Nicholas in spite of herself.

She didn't know whether to feel relieved or saddened that he wasn't present.

Before she could think on it overly much, however, Captain Billings arrived to request the first set.

Alison had danced with the pleasant gentleman, carefully side-stepping the man's various compliments and hints at dancing another together.

When the set was finished, Alison claimed that she was thirsty, and before he could offer to fetch her some punch or ratafia, she'd hurried off in the direction of the refreshments.

That was where she'd been standing when Lord Fulham had approached.

At first, Alison had been wary, remembering Nicholas's fury at finding Fulham with her at Vauxhall Gardens.

But remembering that only made her remember their kiss, which made her heart ache all over again, and that in turn made her more desperate than ever for a distraction.

When Lord Fulham had offered her a glass of champagne, she'd accepted it. Then another, then another.

Now, standing here laughing at his wicked sense of humour, Alison couldn't understand why everyone disliked the man so.

He had sometimes been a little more flirtatious than was entirely appropriate but Nic, or Saint Nic as he was named by Simon, had kissed her until her knees buckled, had held her in his lap, had made her fall utterly, desperately in love with him, and then told her cousin and brother-in-law that he had no interest in her.

So, what was so very bad about Lord Fulham?

He was handsome. He wasn't closed off. He had never criticized her, never called her a spoilt, selfish, brat.

She had no interest in him. Would never marry him. In fact, if she had her way she'd never marry anyone. She would just return to America and pretend this whole year hadn't happened.

Ironic given she'd told Nicholas that pretending

something tragic hadn't happened was no way to heal.

But she knew she would never recover from loving Nic, anyway.

Fulham reached out and ran a finger along the skin exposed by the capped sleeve of her gown.

Alison subtly moved her arm away, ignoring the slight feeling of discomfort.

It was only that she wasn't used to a man being openly affectionate.

And because she wasn't in love with Lord Fulham and didn't crave his touch with a need that bordered on desperation.

"I must say, Miss Langton, it's rather nice seeing you again without your guard dogs. And you seem much more, ah, *relaxed* without them."

Alison laughed with a joviality she didn't quite feel.

"I can't help but feel that you cannot be your true self with them standing watch." He smiled, the expression a touch predatory.

"And I can't help but feel that you have a death wish, since I told you to stay away from her."

Alison whipped around, and there stood Nicholas, six feet of navy-eyed fury staring down at her.

Well, not at her. At Lord Fulham.

Lord Fulham sighed, a small smirk on his face.

"It appears the hound is back," he said to Alison.

She didn't respond, just stared at Nicholas.

Her emotions were tumultuous. Standing in front

of him, she was angry with herself for the depth of love she felt.

Even after all the things he'd said, she wanted to throw herself into his arms.

She wanted to pretend she hadn't heard the things he'd said last night.

But of course, she couldn't.

"Perhaps it is I who wouldn't stay away from him, your grace." She grinned conspiratorially at the viscount by her side.

He threw back his head and laughed whilst Alison's stomach twisted uncomfortably.

The look of shocked hurt on Nicholas's face was excruciating.

Why did he look that way when he didn't want her for himself? Why was he over here acting for all the world like a jealous suitor? Didn't he understand that just pained and confused her all the more?

The scowl stamped on his face now was so similar to the one he used to wear around her, it almost made her nostalgic.

"Alison, dear, perhaps it's time to leave."

Alison shook her head at Amelia.

She didn't know quite why she was acting thus.

The champagne that had been helping to dull the pain slightly was starting to make her head ache, and she was no longer in the mood for dancing, but still she refused.

"I don't want to leave," she said mutinously, acting like the child Nic had once accused her of being. It gave her a perverse sort of pleasure to be behaving this way in front of him. If she were seen in such a manner, she might as well act in such a manner.

"But if you're tired, you and Simon can leave. I'm sure Lord Fulham will escort me home."

"I'd be more than happy to take you home, Miss Langton," he said, his tone setting her teeth on edge.

Maybe she was playing a little too much with fire. But it was better than backing down in front of Nicholas.

"And I'd be more than happy to shoot you," Nicholas said, his voice calm and all the more threatening because of it.

Alison gaped, Lord Fulham gulped, Simon grinned.

"I really think we should leave, Alison, lest Nicholas actually shoot the blighter."

This from Amelia, who didn't seem at all bothered by the threat of death.

"This is ridiculous," Alison snapped, beginning to feel overwhelmed by her confusion around Nic. If she hadn't overheard him last night, she wouldn't even have been speaking to Lord Fulham, let alone flirting outrageously with him. She'd have been dancing in Nic's arms, feeling like she was floating.

But now…

As though the orchestra had read her mind, they

plucked the opening strings of the supper waltz.

Lord Fulham turned his back to Nicholas, Simon, and Amelia.

"Miss Langton," he said. "Would you do me the honour of –"

Nic shot a hand out, grabbing the other man by the lapel and pulling him away from Alison.

"Don't even think about finishing that," he spat.

He pushed Lord Fulham away from him.

Fulham staggered back a few steps, gaining the attention of the people around them.

"Let's go." Nic's tone brooked no argument.

Amelia darted her gaze around the waiting *beau monde,* their eyes wide, their mouths agape.

"Perhaps we should –"

"I'm not going anywhere with you." Alison spoke over Amelia, ignoring what would no doubt have been a very sensible suggestion.

"Alison, dear. We're drawing quite a crowd.

"What the hell is wrong with you?"

Once more, Amelia's reasonable voice fell on deaf ears as Nicholas snapped at Alison, his eyes boring into her.

It was a testament to his anger, Alison knew, that not only would he swear at her, but he would risk causing a scene in front of all Society.

Lord Fulham came forward, his face angry, his cheeks red.

"If you value your life, you'll turn around and walk away," Simon said to the viscount.

Severill had already scampered off the second he'd seen Simon, and the crowd of gentlemen who'd been surrounding Alison had wisely dispersed.

The entire thing was becoming farcical.

Alison looked around, at the smirking Lord Fulham, at the whispering ladies and speculative gentlemen.

At Amelia's uneasy gaze, and Simon's quizzical one.

Finally, at Nic's fury.

And it was suddenly all too much for her.

She was humiliated, heart sore, and tired of the whole thing.

"Alison –" Nic stepped forward, holding a hand out to her.

At the same time, Lord Fulham placed a proprietorial hand on her shoulder.

Suddenly, Nic's fist shot out and connected with Fulham's nose, landing the viscount sprawling on the floor.

All around them, scandalous whispers broke out, ladies' fans fluttering a mile a minute.

Alison glared at him.

He didn't want her, but risking her reputation meant nobody else would either.

"Just leave me alone," she said wearily before turning and rushing from the ballroom.

Chapter Twenty-Nine

N IC HAD NO idea what had happened just now. He was aware of the furor he'd just created, but he was past caring.

Something was wrong with Alison, and he was going to find out what it was.

He went to rush after her, stopping only when he felt Simon's hand on his shoulder.

Turning around, impatient with his friend, he watched as Simon bent to whisper something in Amelia's ear, and with a quick nod she dashed off in a flurry of lilac skirts.

"Simon," Nic warned. "Let me go."

"What are you doing?" Simon asked, dropping his hand, his tone low enough that the listening ears around them couldn't hear.

Fulham had staggered to his feet, and Nic felt a perverse pleasure in the blood staining his once white cravat and lawn shirt.

"I'm going after Alison," Nic said impatiently. "Can't you see she's upset?"

"Yes, I can. And I can see that you're the reason."

This brought Nic up short.

"Last night, you said nothing was going on. You said you had no intentions toward her."

"I know what I said," Nic spat in exacerbation.

"So, you lied?"

"No! I just – I didn't know what I was doing. What I wanted."

Simon studied him silently for a moment.

"Do you love her?"

Nic had wanted Alison to be the first person he told, but he wasn't sure Simon would let him go if his friend thought he wasn't being honourable. The irony of the devil checking the saint's behaviour wasn't lost on Nic.

He nodded. Just once, but it was enough.

Simon smirked.

"What?" Nic demanded.

"Oh, nothing. I'm just enjoying the fact that after years of Robert and James warning me away from every female of their acquaintance, Saint Nic here swoops in and seduces one right under their noses."

"I didn't seduce –"

"Go," Simon laughingly interrupted Nic's protestations. "Given how up in the boughs Alison looked, I'm not sure how long my wife will be able to keep her here."

"HOW LONG DOES a bloody carriage take?"

Alison scowled at Amelia's sudden grin.

"What's so funny?" she asked.

"Nothing," Amelia said. "That was just a terribly English swear word. I forget sometimes that you're an American."

"Yes, well you'll remember soon enough."

"Oh? And why is that?" Amelia asked.

The sound of a carriage arriving momentarily distracted Alison, and she was relieved to see the conveyance stamped with the Dashford coat of arms.

The sooner she got away from here, and Nicholas, the better.

"Because I'm going home," she said.

It was the best thing to do. There was nothing in England for her now; she was sure of it.

"What?" Amelia gasped. "Alison, you cannot be serious."

Alison would be miserable at home with her disinterested family, of that she had no doubt. But being miserable with an ocean separating her from the source of her desolation seemed rather palatable at that moment.

"There's nothing here for me, Amelia," she said miserably.

"Nothing?" her friend asked gently.

To Alison's horror, she felt tears fill her eyes at the young countess's question.

"You know?" she asked.

Amelia shrugged apologetically.

Wonderful. Now everyone knew Alison was a fool who'd fallen in love with someone who didn't want her. And never would.

"When I fell in love with Simon," Amelia said softly, "I was more miserable than I'd ever been in my life."

Alison remembered the time well.

She'd only met Simon and Amelia as they were falling in love. It had been obvious to everyone around them that they were besotted with each other. But for some reason, the two of them couldn't seem to find their way to each other.

It had all come right in the end, however. A fate that did not await Alison.

"I couldn't understand why Adeline read all those stupid novels about love," Amelia said of her younger sister, now happily married herself. "To me, it was the worst thing a person could experience. And I'd just finished researching medieval plagues."

Alison smiled in spite of herself at her beautiful, bookish friend.

"And look at me now," Amelia continued.

"It won't be like that for me, Amelia," Alison sniffled.

"Whyever not?" The countess reached out and gripped Alison's hand.

Alison would dearly love to pour her heart out to the kindly brunette beside her. But Nic's story wasn't Alison's to tell.

So instead of being able to confess that the man she loved was in love with a ghost, she could only shake her head sadly.

"Oh, my dear, it will all turn out well. I'm sure of it."

Amelia watched Alison closely before nodding as though coming to a decision.

"Let's go back and find Simon so we can get you home," she said softly.

Alison nodded and turned with her friend to go back inside.

She looked up and froze.

Nic was standing there gazing intently at her, an unreadable look on his face.

"I'll just – go and fetch Simon," Amelia said hesitantly, giving Alison's hand one more squeeze before hurrying up the steps.

Nic stopped her, bending to whisper something to her, his eyes never leaving Alison, who stood trapped in his gaze.

Amelia looked swiftly back at Alison before she nodded then turned and continued up the steps and into the house.

Nic walked toward Alison slowly, carefully.

"Are you well?" he asked, his voice quiet and even, as though he hadn't been swearing at her and punching viscounts only moments ago.

"Not particularly," she said wearily.

The fight had gone out of her.

In the ballroom, she'd had her anger as a shield against him. Her indignation that he had dismissed her so easily to her family. Her resentment that, try as she might, she would never live up to the perfection of his first love.

Ciara had been a maid, after all. And Nicholas had loved her so much he'd been willing to give up everything.

And though Alison had thought she could live with him just caring for her a little, she was coming to realise that wouldn't be enough for her.

She wanted someone to love her enough to give up everything for her. She wanted someone to love her as much as she loved Nic. As much as he loved someone else.

It was tragic.

But she couldn't help it any more than she could help how she felt about him.

"I'm sorry," he said, stepping closer so that now there were only inches between them. "I lost my temper. It seems I find it hard to control myself around you, in more ways than one."

She had no idea what to say to such a thing, so she said nothing.

"Lord Fulham is not safe for you to be around, Alison."

Alison snorted. She couldn't help it. The only one dangerous to her was the man standing in front of her.

He frowned disapprovingly.

"I'm serious," he said. "He is not to be trusted. If you knew what I knew, what we all know about him –"

"You just don't like him," Alison shot back. "He's only ever been nice to me."

She thought of the times Lord Fulham made her uncomfortable but ruthlessly dismissed them.

"He's being nice to you because he wants to bed you," Nic said bluntly. "And, no, I don't like him. I never did. Now, I hate him with a viciousness I didn't know I was capable of. But I'm man enough to admit my jealousy probably has a lot to do with that."

Alison felt her jaw drop.

He seemed so sincere, so affectionate. She could almost believe that he cared about her. But last night he'd told his friends that he didn't.

Her head ached with her circuitous thoughts.

"I'm tired," she said. "And my head hurts. I'm going home as soon as Amelia gets back with Simon, so –"

"Amelia isn't coming back with Simon," Nicholas interrupted smoothly.

"But, but she said I could leave," Alison said,

sounding petulant even to her own ears.

"And you can. I'm taking you home."

"No!" The protestation was out of her mouth before she even realised.

Once again, Nic's eyes flashed with hurt confusion.

But he had no right to be hurt. Not when he'd said that he didn't want anything to do with her.

"Alison, I don't understand what is going on here tonight. Yesterday we were – well, I thought we were –"

He paused, seeming to search for words to say.

But she couldn't stand there and hear this. She couldn't listen to reminders of yesterday. Not when it had meant something different to them both.

"Nicholas, I'm glad you told me about Ciara and about your son," she said sadly. "I'm glad you shared with me all the wonderful work you do and why you do it. But we're different people, you and I. We want very different things."

He flinched as though she'd slapped him.

"What does that mean?" he asked woodenly, his face and tone expressionless.

But she knew him so well now. It didn't fool her.

He hid behind his mask of calm stoicism. Whatever he was feeling, he was going to hide it from her. Just like he'd hidden how he'd really been feeling when she'd sat in his arms.

"It means that I came to London looking for something, and I don't think I'm going to find here. I thought I could, but I can't."

He opened his mouth to speak once more, but she needed to leave before she broke down completely in front of him.

"It means I'm going home. Back to America. Back where I belong."

"Alison, no."

He reached out and clasped the tops of her arms, shaking her gently.

"You cannot mean that. I want –"

"I don't care what you want, Nic." She yanked herself free from his grasp.

Her anger reappeared swift and scorching.

"You made it very clear last night what you *don't* want, and that's me."

"What are you talking about? I never said –"

"What? You never said that I'm a spoilt, selfish brat?"

His cheeks paled, and she got a twisted pleasure in seeing his reaction.

"You never said that you warned Robert about how I would be trouble? You never said that you had no intentions toward me?"

To her horror, she felt tears fill her eyes, and try as she might, she could not stop them falling.

Nic's black oath summed up her own feelings rather well.

"I was so happy yesterday," she continued. The

words came of their own volition. Streaming from her as though her broken heart were purging itself. "I thought that perhaps you were growing to care about me. Let me in."

She reached a hand up and impatiently dashed away her tears.

"I was stupid – naïvely imagining a life together, where I would be by your side in St. Giles and any-where else you were. Where we would spend our days in love and helping those less fortunate."

His expression was stricken, but he didn't move. Didn't speak. Merely stared at her. And that felt as though her heart were ripping clean out of her chest.

It was further proof that she was an idiot.

God, how she wished he would say he wanted that, too.

"But last night, I finally accepted what you really think of me. I finally accepted that you will never love me, not like I love you."

Perhaps she shouldn't have told him. But Alison didn't feel like she had anything left to lose by being honest.

"But I can't make you love me. I can't even make you like me." She laughed bitterly.

Dropping her gaze to her feet, she let the tears come unchecked now.

Taking a deep breath, she lifted her eyes to his.

"And I can't compete with a ghost."

Chapter Thirty

"SHE WON'T COME out of her room again."

"And Nic won't come out of his house."

Robert and James looked at each other, matching expressions of concern on their faces.

"You're sure nothing happened at that ball?" Robert turned to Simon now, who had been listening quietly to the gentlemen's exchange.

"Nothing at all," he lied smoothly. "Apart from the fact that I thought Nic would actually kill Fulham. Shame he didn't."

Nic stood just outside Robert's study, listening to their exchange.

He didn't mean to eavesdrop, obviously.

But when he'd heard James mention Alison, he'd been frozen to the spot.

Last night had been the worst night of his life.

Alison had told him that she loved him. That she thought he didn't love her, too. When everything in his life now seemed meaningless without her.

He never should have let her get into that carriage alone.

He never should have granted her wish to be alone.

Drinking himself into a stupor during the night hadn't helped.

Pacing up and down the empty, vast halls of his townhouse hadn't helped.

Nothing had.

Because he didn't need brandy, or to be locked in his own miserable thoughts.

He needed Alison, needed her more than the air he breathed.

But needing her, loving her, and being worthy of her – being whole and absolutely sure of what he wanted – they were two different things.

Whilst he'd poured pot after pot of dark, strong coffee down his throat that morning, Nic had been hastily throwing together plans.

And now, he was ready to start implementing them. Because he never wanted to upset her or make her doubt his feelings for her ever again.

His palms were sweating, his breath ragged, and he could feel something akin to panic begin to prickle at the edge of his mind.

Never had he thought he would be able to confide in his friends, able to tell them he'd been living a lie for the past ten years. But now, for the first time since they'd become men, he was about to tell them that this time, he was the one who needed help.

He walked into the room, his eyes scanning the

faces of his closest friends.

Each one of them stared back at him.

Finally, James broke the somewhat awkward silence. "What the hell happened to you?" he blurted.

"You look like Simon after one of his infamous nights," Robert added.

"Thank you. Really. I'm touched." This from Simon, who stood and nodded subtly to Nic.

He hadn't told Robert and James what Nic had confided last night. Hadn't told them about Nic's love for Alison.

It was Nic's story to tell. But it wasn't the only one.

Taking a deep breath, Nic looked each one of them in the eye.

"I'm in love with Alison," he said simply, clearly. "I'm sorry that I didn't tell you. And I'm sorry that I lied when you asked me what I intended. But – I wasn't myself. I wasn't thinking straight."

He swore softly to himself.

"I haven't been thinking straight for weeks."

He swallowed a sudden lump in his throat and shrugged helplessly.

"I love her," he repeated.

There was a brief silence.

"Well, obviously," James finally said.

"Yes, if you're going to make a dramatic announcement, Nic, you might want to make it something that we didn't already know." Rob grinned.

"He told me yesterday," Simon said smugly.

Nic could only stare at them.

"You know?" he asked.

"Of course, we know. We have eyes."

"The question is, what are you going to do about it?"

"Well, as to that – she's angry with me."

"Which is presumably why she's locked herself away?"

"I'm sorry about that," Nic said.

"It's fine," Robert said quickly. "I sent Abigail out into a storm."

"Senna got shot because of me."

They all looked to Simon.

He shrugged.

"Amelia has to put up with me every single day."

Nic laughed along with the others, his chest loosening slightly.

But the hard part was yet to come.

"Are you here to propose?" Rob asked. "Because I'm not sure she'll talk to you"

"I'm not here to talk to Alison," Nic said, even though he physically ached to go to her. "I'm here to talk to you. To all of you."

ALISON'S HEART THUNDERED loudly as she sat anxiously

awaiting the arrival of a servant.

Eliza had told her that Lord Barnbury had arrived over an hour ago, and still she had yet to be summoned to Robert.

Her heart, which apparently couldn't learn its lesson, had burst with elation when she'd heard that he'd arrived, and though she tried not to, she couldn't help but wonder if he were here for her.

However, nobody had called for her, and now she wondered if perhaps he was here to tell tales.

Perhaps he was here to reiterate to Robert that he'd been right about her.

That she was scandalous, flirting with viscounts and telling dukes she loved them. Following gentlemen into the underbelly of London, and dancing barefoot in fountains.

She half expected Robert, himself, to come thundering up the stairs and ship her back to the Americas.

Well, good, she said to herself with a conviction she didn't feel, *I want to go home anyway.*

The hours ticked on.

Alison had been determined to stay in her room, hiding from everyone.

But curiosity was getting the better of her.

Finally, she could bear it no longer.

Moving as quietly as possible, she slipped out of her rooms and moved swiftly along the corridor to the staircase.

Just as she reached the top, the door to Robert's study opened and Nicholas swept out, moving quickly toward the foyer.

She didn't make a sound. Alison was sure of it.

But just as a waiting footman swung open the door, he stopped.

Spinning around, his eyes scanned the hallway before moving up and finding hers.

Alison's breath caught as his navy-blue gaze bored into her.

She stood frozen, unable to move or look away.

Her heart was hammering, begging him to come to her. To say something, at least.

But apart from a quick flash of some powerful emotion, his expression remained calm and unmoved.

After a torturous moment, he bowed briefly, turned on his heel and, without saying a word, walked away.

Chapter Thirty-One

"WHO IS THE note from, dear?"

Alison looked up from the missive in her hand to see Abigail staring curiously at her.

It had been two days since Nic had been here.

Two days of complete silence from him.

Alison hadn't left the house. She'd declined all invitations to parties and balls, refused to accompany Abigail at afternoon calls, and begged Abby to make her excuses during her *At Home.*

Last night, she'd announced that she intended to return home as soon as the Season was done.

Truth be told, she didn't want to even continue the Season, but it would take time to pack everything up, so she could be patient.

Especially because she didn't particularly want to go home.

The truth was she didn't particularly want to do *anything.*

London had lost its appeal. Ever since her visit to the children's home, the superficial nature of most members of the *ton* irritated her.

All the parties were the same; all the people were the same. The gentlemen were either lascivious or sycophantic. The ladies fawning or snide.

She didn't like it, she had come to realise.

Dinner parties, balls, and soirees were fun and entertaining, but in small doses. The daily events were taking their toll on her.

Abigial was surprised to find that Alison was less than impressed with the glittering world of the *beau monde,* but Alison was as surprised as her sister.

Coming to England, she had been full sure that this life was the one she'd wanted.

Now, just like so many other things, that had changed.

Nicholas Fyfe was to blame for that, too.

And now she'd received this letter.

"I-it's from one of the children I met at the home that Ni– that Lord Barnbury sponsors," she said quickly.

She wouldn't say that it was a home the duke frequented.

Much as he had broken her heart, Alison wouldn't betray Nicholas's secret.

"One of the children? How nice," Abigail said blandly. "What does it say?"

"I had promised that I would play for them and maybe teach them to play themselves." Alison swallowed hard.

She never should have made such a promise. She had done so thinking that she would spend lots of time there.

"Apparently, the duke had a pianoforte delivered yesterday and they want me to come and try it."

"Well, you must certainly go," Abby said quickly. "You cannot let the poor, orphaned children down, can you?"

Alison scowled.

"No, I suppose I can't," she agreed reluctantly.

She didn't *want* to let the children down. But she really didn't want to see Nicholas, either.

"Why don't you finish your breakfast, and we'll call for the carriage to take us there."

Alison gaped at her sister.

She wanted to go to St. Giles, just so Alison could play a pianoforte?

"Um, I'm not sure that's a good idea," Alison said now. "It's not the sort of place we should go to alone."

"Isn't that the place *you* went to alone?" Abby blinked at her.

"Well, yes," Alison said. "But, I promised –"

"You promised what?"

Her heart twisted painfully as she remembered her conversation with Nic.

Only you.

"Never mind," she said dully. "But we really shouldn't go unescorted," she said. "We should ask

Robert."

"Ask me what?" The door to the breakfast room opened and Robert walked in, bending to kiss Abby's head as he walked by her chair.

"Alison has had a note from some of the children at an orphanage in St. Giles and wants to go and visit. We thought that it might be best if you came with us."

"It's not best, it's imperative. You cannot go anywhere near that place without me or Nic. Not ever."

Robert's intensity would have taken Alison by surprise if she hadn't seen with her own eyes just how dangerous those streets were. Truth be told, she would be glad to have her intimidating brother-in-law with her.

"We should ready ourselves then," Abigail said, ignoring Robert's protectiveness.

Alison nodded, following her sister out of the breakfast room.

The last thing she wanted was to go anywhere near the place that was so much a part of Nicholas.

But what choice did she have?

THREE HOURS AND ten songs later, the children of the home were finally convinced to have a rest.

Alison's fingers must be aching by now, but Nic had yet to see her grimace or complain.

All morning he'd watched her charm and enchant the children. They were as drawn to her as he was, as everyone around her was.

Nic's heart ached when he thought of her believing that he didn't love her.

Of course, he loved her. How could he do anything *but* love her?

He'd kept his distance, anxious to do this right. He didn't want her storming off the second she'd arrived.

As Rob had promised, he'd accompanied Alison to the door of the home.

His friend's surprise had been evident when he'd entered Nic's small, cramped office. There were papers everywhere. Reports on the finances, the children, their wants and needs.

"I still can't quite believe you kept your involvement in all of this so well hidden," he'd said.

The day Nic had confessed his history to his friends, they'd sat in Robert's study for hours. It had been one of the most difficult conversations of Nic's life but afterwards, the relief at finally letting his surrogate family in had been palpable. He'd felt a decade younger as he'd unburdened himself to Simon, James, and Robert.

And as he'd hurried away to put into place everything he wanted for Alison, he'd sensed her there.

Her soul called to his own, Nic was sure of it.

Even today when she'd arrived, he'd felt her presence in the air.

Seeing her standing forlornly at the top of Robert's staircase had been gut-wrenching, especially because he couldn't go to her as he wanted, hold her as he wanted.

But it was imperative that he do this right. He wouldn't go near her until he had everything in place to show her, once and for all, that she was his everything.

If Nic had left Alison in any doubt as to how much she meant to him, he intended to fix that today.

Mrs. Cafferty bustled the children out of the newly appointed music room and hurried them along to the dining hall, with Robert and Abigail laughingly helping to herd them.

And then, there was just Alison.

She still sat on the piano bench by the window, her hair gleaming gold in the afternoon sunlight, the summer breeze playing with soft tendrils in a way that made Nic itch to touch them.

She looked beautiful.

She looked miserable.

And Nic vowed to himself that if he were lucky enough to make her his, he would never cause her unhappiness again.

"They are quite the little taskmasters."

Her head snapped up at his comment, her impossibly blue eyes wide.

"I don't mind," she said eventually. "In fact, I love it. When I go home, I'll be sure to continue it in the local orphanage."

Nic's heart thudded painfully at her talk of leaving.

He couldn't imagine her going home. He couldn't imagine her anywhere but by his side, where she belonged.

"You like the pianoforte?" He nodded toward the instrument, stepping further into the room.

"It's beautiful." She turned to run her gaze over it, lovingly caressing the ebony and ivory keys with her fingertips. "You are very good to them."

"It's nothing." He shrugged. "It's the very least I can do."

She smiled a little but didn't speak.

Nic kept walking until he'd stopped in front of her, peering down at her.

"May I?" he asked, indicating the bench.

She frowned up at him.

"It's a little small," she said softly.

"Ah, so it is." He nodded sagely. "Perhaps you would agree to join me for a walk in the garden?"

He could see her searching for a way to say no, and it killed him that she didn't want to spend time alone with him.

Though after what she'd heard the other night, he couldn't blame her.

If he lived a hundred years, he'd never forgive himself for hurting her like that.

"Please, Alison," he said softly, before she could refuse.

She heaved a sigh then jutted out her chin determinedly.

"Fine," she said dully. "Let's go."

She plucked a rose-coloured shawl from the edge of the bench, folding it over her arm, then walked stiffly from the room.

Nicholas felt a niggle of worry at how distant she was being.

But it wouldn't stop him trying.

Nothing would stop him from trying.

Once outside, she placed the shawl over the short sleeves of her invory muslin dress.

"Where do you want to walk to?" she asked.

"I wanted to show you something."

She didn't speak, merely nodded and waited for him to lead the way.

"You know, I've never been to the Americas," Nic said conversationally.

She blinked up at him, and Nic had to clench his fists to keep from reaching for her.

"I've never really been anywhere outside of London since Ciara died."

He was watching her so closely that he noticed the tiniest flinch at Ciara's name.

She truly believed he still loved Ciara.

"I think I would find it strange to leave London and all of the places I do my work at."

They'd been walking slowly, past the fountain, past the flower beds and vegetable patches, past the small orchard of apple trees.

Now, he reached out and drew her to a stop.

"But if you really want to go back, I could get used to it."

Chapter Thirty-Two

ALISON COULD ONLY stare at Nicholas as his words sank in.

Did he mean –?

What *did* he mean?

Instead of expanding, however, he turned to look at a small, white stone pillar.

Alison saw a cross embedded in it.

"We buried Ciara here," Nic said quietly.

She snapped her gaze up to him, but his entire focus was on the monument in front of them.

How could she be noticing the strength of his chin, the curve of his lashes, the lock of chestnut hair that fell across his brow when he was standing at the grave of his love?

She was a disgrace.

"This was where the tenement I found her in stood. I had the entire street demolished so I could build the home. I moved the residents to one of the houses I purchased nearby."

Alison didn't understand why he was telling her this.

And what had he meant about getting used to America?

"It seemed right that she should find rest here, where she had suffered so much."

Alison nodded, and because she hated the idea of him being in pain, reached out a hand to rest gently on his arm.

"I forgave myself years ago for Ciara's fate, or at least I thought I had. It was only when you spoke to me about it that I realised I'd pushed it away rather than dealt with it. Blocked my grief instead of healing from it."

She dropped her hand, clasping her fingers together.

She had no idea why Nic had brought her here, why he was telling her this. And every one of his words cut like a knife. But if he needed to talk, then she would listen.

"You made me see that I needed to open myself up to the feelings that I'd buried."

Alison would have laughed if it weren't so tragic; she had reawakened his feelings for Ciara, all the while falling in love with him.

"I told Robert, James, and Simon about her and about my son."

"You did?" she asked in amazement.

"I did. And you were right – it was better for me to let them in. They would have helped me then – they want to help me now."

"Help you?"

Nic suddenly turned to gaze at her, his eyes heated and intense.

"Come on," he said, grasping her hand and pulling her back through the garden.

She should have pulled her hand back. Touching him now would only make it hurt more later.

But she kept it right where it was. Kept holding on.

Nic continued walking until they were back at the fountain.

"You said the other day that you couldn't compete with a ghost."

Alison's heart twisted at the reminder of her words.

The reminder that she'd told him she loved him like a great, big, idiot.

"And you're right. You can't compete with a ghost."

Alison dropped her gaze to the ground.

She'd known that. Of course, she'd known it. So, why did it hurt so much?

Her eyes filled with tears once more.

"Or rather." Nic placed a finger under her chin, lifting her face, forcing her gaze to his. "Nobody and nothing could compete with you," he said. "Not a ghost, not a living, breathing human being. Not my charities. Not my friends. Nothing compares, Alison. Nothing comes close."

Alison's heart tripped and stuttered.

She didn't know what this meant; she was afraid to guess.

"I don't understand," she whispered, her throat tight and painful.

"You think I'm still in love with Ciara." Nic's eyes bored into hers, suspiciously bright. "You couldn't be more wrong," he said. "Ciara was special to me. In my naïve youth, I was sure I loved her."

He moved to sit on the edge of the fountain, pulling her down to sit beside him, keeping her hand clasped in his own.

"And for the past ten years, I convinced myself that the reason I'd never loved was because my heart had been too broken. Or that I didn't have the ability to love anymore."

He reached up and brushed at a tear she hadn't even noticed falling with his thumb.

"And then you came along." He smiled. "You were a storm, raging into my life and causing chaos. I didn't know what to do about the feelings you stirred up inside me, so powerful, so strong. Like nothing I'd ever felt before."

Alison couldn't breathe, afraid that if she made even the smallest sound or movement, he would stop saying these amazing, unbelievable things.

"I tried to convince myself I hated you. Then I tried to tell myself that it was nothing more than an attraction to a beautiful woman. You're the most beautiful woman in the world." He smiled wryly. "How could I not be attracted to you?"

He tucked a golden curl behind her ear.

"Of course, then you went and ruined my carefully cultivated opinion of you. Instead of being spoilt and selfish and frivolous, you are kind-hearted and loving, with the most generous, giving spirit of anyone I know."

The tears fell freely; there was no stemming them.

"I realised then that I absolutely had the ability to love. To love fiercely and with my whole heart. It was just that I'd never been in love before, Alison. Not even with Ciara. I did love her, cared for her. But all-consuming, life-changing love? That was new to me. I hate what happened to her, hate that because of me she lost her life in the most awful way."

He swallowed hard, his eyes glinting in the sun-light.

"I brought you to her gravesite because it's been a cornerstone for me for many years. A reminder of why I do what I do. And I want no part of me hidden from you."

He took a deep breath before continuing.

"And there's not a day that goes by when I don't feel helpless, and angry, and desperately sad that my baby died."

His eyes dulled momentarily with a pain she

couldn't even begin to imagine.

"But the love I have for you – it consumes me. It's everything. I felt torn at first, wondering how I could walk away from all of this to be the husband you deserve."

Her heart stopped dead at the word husband.

"Then I was faced with the prospect of being apart from you, and I almost lost my mind. I would gladly give all of this up. If you want to go back to the Americas, I only ask that you allow me to come, too."

"Nicholas," she finally managed to choke. "I don't –"

"Please," he interrupted suddenly, desperately. "Please, don't tell me you don't love me. I know it took me too long to get here, but I swear to you, I will spend my life making up for the hurt I've caused you. Telling Robert, James, and Simon, spending the last two days getting all of my affairs in order here – it's all been so that I can be with you completely and forever. However you want me. Wherever you are."

"I do love you." She sniffed, too simply to convey what she was feeling inside. "So very much."

He reached out and clasped her cheeks.

"Thank God," he whispered before capturing her mouth in a desperate, explosive kiss.

When he eventually let her up for air, pressing his forehead against her own, their breathing laboured, Alison was able to gather her wits enough to speak.

Though she couldn't quite believe this was really,

truly, happening, there were important things they needed to get straightened out.

"Nic, I don't want you to go to America," she said, and the look of pain that flashed across his face was proof, if she needed it, that he'd meant every wonderful word he'd said.

"I don't want you to leave here, this place, this work that is so important to you."

"But –"

She reached out and placed a finger against his lips, becoming momentarily distracted by his pupils dilating.

But before she could allow herself to be distracted by – well, *that* – they needed to talk.

"It's too important," she continued. "To you and to the people who rely on you."

"I won't leave them in the lurch," he interjected. "I've made provisions, put people in place."

"But they want *you*" she argued gently. "The Saint of St. Giles."

He scowled at the moniker, and she laughed softly.

"This is so much a part of you, Nic. I don't want you to leave it. I just want to be a part of it, too."

He frowned, and she knew he was going to argue.

"I'll never be safer than when I'm with you," she headed off his argument before he could even make it. "And as I promised you before, I'll never come here with anyone else."

She leaned forward and placed a gentle kiss on his lips, pulling back before she could get carried away.

"Only you."

NIC'S HEART HAMMERED with love, and pride, and every possible emotion as he watched Alison read yet another story to the children before Mrs. Cafferty and the maids bundled them all off to bed.

As soon as they were done, he pulled her along the quiet corridor to his office.

Nobody disturbed him there, and for what he had in mind, they definitely did not want to be disturbed.

Earlier Senna, James, Amelia, and Simon had arrived, and he had proudly shown them the facility that he'd walked Robert and Abigail around only hours before.

They'd all played with the children, Poppy having a grand time with girls her own age, and eaten the same simple food prepared for the children and staff.

He truly had the best of friends.

He could regret not telling them of this part of his life sooner, but Nic had learned not to live a life of regrets, and so he would focus instead on being happy in the more active role they all vowed to take in his work here.

Robert, once he'd learned that Alison had agreed to

marry Nic, was happy to allow her to stay longer, knowing that Nic would take care of her like nobody else.

They'd all gone home, with yet more shouts of felicitations. The staff had taken the children to settle them for the night, and finally, Nic and Alison were alone.

As soon as Nic shut the door of his office, he pulled his fiancé into his arms and kissed her as though his life depended on it.

And so it did, in a way. His heart, his soul, his everything revolved around the woman in his arms.

"You know," he said, sitting down in his large, leather chair, the only luxury he allowed himself here, pulling her to sit in his lap. "When we first met, it took every bit of me not to love you."

"And now?" She grinned, the look causing desire, hot and molten, to awaken inside him.

"Now, you just take every bit of me," he said softly.

Outside, the streets of St. Giles raged with danger, peril, and menace.

But within these walls, its children slept safe and well.

And in his office, the Saint of St. Giles set about proving to his fiancé just how much of a sinner he could be.

THE END.

Epilogue

"PAPA, PLEASE, PLEASE let me go. Sarah's father is a boring old fuddy-duddy. Nothing is going to happen."

"I seem to recall you calling me a boring old fuddy-duddy," Nic whispered in Alison's ear as they watched the exchange between Poppy and James.

"I cannot believe you still bring that up, ten years later." She rolled her eyes before relaxing against him, his arm moving at once to gather her closer.

"Poppy, I told you already, I will speak to Lord Fantan and make my decision then. You've plenty of time to visit Bath, you're only eighteen."

Poppy opened her mouth, no doubt to argue again, but seemed to think better of it.

And with a smile on her face that her adoptive father, as well as all of her uncles, had always been powerless against, she leaned down to kiss his cheek.

"Thank you, Papa." She grinned before hurrying off, her blonde curls bouncing in the weak, winter sun.

"I didn't say, yes," James grumbled as Senna reached out to pat his hand.

"You might as well have, darling," she laughed, one eye on their boisterous twins who were engaging in an ever-rougher stick fight. "Thomas, Rose, please be careful," she called.

Thomas nodded dutifully, but Rose, her red hair the exact shade of her mama's, rolled her eyes and kept going.

She was a termagant, of that there was no doubt.

Lottie rushed over with an oversized book in her hand and immediately plonked herself beside her Aunt Amelia, who leaned forward to admire whatever it was the studious girl had discovered amongst its pages.

Lottie showed every sign of being as bookish as the countess, whereas her own children, Michael and Helena, were more interested in hunting and fishing.

Amelia blamed their father, who was currently holding court with a group of the children. Michael and Helena, Robert's son Jacob, along with Nic and Alison's daughters Lily and Ella were in Simon's thrall completely as he recounted the tale of a tiger attack on one of Amelia's expeditions, complete with re-enactment of said attack so they could all take turns pretending to shoot him.

Nic and Alison's son, who was shier than his sisters, sat by a small pond, riveted by the fish his Uncle Robert was pointing out.

They had all travelled to Montvale to enjoy some time together before James and Senna took Poppy to

London for her come out.

They would all go to Town for the Season, of course.

Ostensibly to lend Poppy support and ensure she was a success.

Though the ladies were well aware the gentlemen were going more to keep an eye on her possible suitors than anything else.

Abigail appeared, calling the group inside to ready themselves for dinner.

Though it was winter, it had been quite mild, and the weather was just starting to cool.

The children all dashed ahead, their nurses and governesses awaiting their arrival.

Once they'd eaten, their respective parents would put them to bed.

It was always a chaotic, noisy, but fun-filled experience, each couple shirking the *ton* tradition of leaving the care of their children to the staff.

Later, when the children were sleeping, and the gentlemen had finished their port, the eight friends gathered in the drawing room of Montvale Hall.

The room was decorated just as it had been ten years ago.

Given that the late dowager duchess had loved the room like this, Abigail had been loathe to change it.

"It's hard to believe," she said now, "that it was so long ago that I first came here."

"Yes, and Robert was such a grumpy bastard," James laughed, earning a playful slap from his wife.

"A monster through and through," Nic agreed with a grin.

"Anyone would have looked monstrous to you, Saint Nic," Simon teased. "You even gave our Angel here a run for his money in the goodness stakes."

"And anyone would have looked angelic next to your devilish ways," Rob said.

"I wonder, will any of our boys take after me in that respect?" Simon asked thoughtfully, earning laughing denials and objections from the rest of the group.

"Well, whatever way they turn out, we can only hope that they remain as close as they are now. That they remain a family. And that, whether a sinner or a saint, they always stick together," Nic said, his calm voice quieting the faux argument.

Above them, their children slept soundly, each of them destined to carry on their fathers' legacies. Some of them sinners. And some of them saints. But all of them determined to stick together through thick and thin, as their fathers had before them.

THE END.

Thank you for reading *The Sint of St. Giles!* If you enjoyed this story please leave a quick review on your favorite book retailer. Reviews help other readers determine to try my books or not, and I love reading what you thought! If you want to learn about my new releases, or when my books go on sale, please follow me on BookBub, or subscribe to my newsletter.

Keep reading for a special preview of *The Monster of Montvale of Hall*, the first book in the Saints & Sinners series!

The Monster of Montvale Hall
BY
NADINE MILLARD

Prologue

"STOP RUNNING SO fast. I can't keep up."

Robert Forsythe ignored the cries of his little sister, choosing instead to increase his pace as he ran toward the river.

"Ignore her," he yelled to his fellow escapees, his three best friends from Eton. Each of them the son and heir of a powerful Peer. Each of them determined to enjoy this precious time outside where they didn't have to be students, didn't have to be heirs to powerful titles, and didn't have to learn anything of their future responsibilities.

While staying at Robert's home for the Easter break from school, they all wanted to just be children. Just for a little while. Even though they were on the unsteady cusp of manhood.

And Robert didn't want Gina ruining it for them, slowing them down. It was irritating in the extreme to have his stubborn little sister following them around. James's brother, Thomas, was only a year or two older than Gina and he hadn't come after them. He'd stayed behind, like he'd been told to do. Gina would never do as she was told!

It had been storming for days, wind and rain lashing against the window panes of Montvale Hall, making it impossible for the boys to get outside.

The young marquess had never been one for sitting still and had been driven mad being cooped up inside. Though nobody could ever say that the Hall, the seat of his father, The Duke of Montvale, was small enough to feel cooped up in.

Still, there was only so much sport to be had in the cavernous halls filled with irreplaceable family heirlooms.

Even today, the winds were still a force to be reckoned with. But since it was dry, the duchess had agreed to let the boys out for a little while.

"Stay away from the river," she had warned, her tone brooking no argument.

The river current was, according to Mama, dangerously strong after inclement weather and so, of course, that was the first place a group of fourteen-year-old boys would head.

Growing up rarely hearing the word "no" lent them

all a false sense of confidence in their own sensibilities.

"Bobby, *please.*"

Robert swung back to face his sister, his grey eyes flashing with the frustration that only an older brother could feel.

"Gina, get back to the house," he yelled over the howling of the wind.

The sky had darkened ominously even as they'd tramped across the grounds of the estate.

"Robert, perhaps we should go back."

Robert turned to face his closest friend, the future Marquess of Avondale, with a grimace.

"Don't be silly, James. We've been stuck indoors for days."

"The weather is turning quite badly, and Gina shouldn't be out in this."

Robert's temper flared. No, Gina shouldn't be out in this. But Gina wasn't *supposed* to be out in this.

"The others are gone ahead," Robert said mutinously, pointing to where his two other close friends, Simon and Nicholas, could be seen headed toward the brook.

James looked hesitantly from Gina to their friends.

"You go ahead," he said finally. "I'll walk Gina back to the Hall and come back to you."

Robert felt an immediate swell of anger. It was so typical of James, the golden boy. Always doing what he should. Always doing what was right.

Robert hated that James made him feel lacking or not good enough.

"No, she's my baby sister," he bit out, resentful of the duty that fell to him.

"I'm not a baby," Gina shouted mutinously, and Robert had to smile in spite of himself.

In truth, even though he felt like he could happily ring her neck at times, he doted on Gina and had his mood not been so foul from being stuck inside for days at a time, he likely would have indulged her from the start.

"Gina, if I let you come, you must stay by my side. Do you understand?"

His sister's light grey eyes, so like his own, lit up at once, and he allowed himself a brief smile.

"I really don't think that's a good idea," James insisted.

Robert's stomach flip-flopped with uneasiness. Mama would have his head if she found out he'd allowed Gina to accompany them to the river – they weren't supposed to be headed there, either.

Nonetheless, he had always looked after her, and he would do so now.

"Come, James, by the time we get her back to the Hall the others will be wanting to return. We can watch her well enough."

James hesitated again, annoying Robert once more.

In truth, he and James were the best of friends with

only months between them in age. But James was just so *good* all the time. Mama often joked that Robert was the anti-James, though Robert wasn't sure how much she was actually joking.

Robert's mother was James's godmother. And when James's mother had died in childbirth whilst the boys were toddlers, the Duchess of Montvale had become a sort of surrogate aunt to James, and he spent more time at Montvale than at his own future seat, Avondale Abbey.

Fathers, the boys had been informed, were not cut out to look after children.

Finally, after what seemed an age, James relented.

"Fine, come along then Gina." James smiled indulgently at his little honorary cousin. "If you get soaked to the bone or catch a chill, we shall just blame Robert."

Gina clapped her hands excitedly and then dashed off after Simon and Nicholas.

"She will be a handful when she's older," Robert said, not entirely sure what that meant, but he'd heard his father say so enough times to think it must be true.

"Yes, and she will also be your problem," James said with a laugh.

The two boys raced off after Gina, pushing, shoving, and jostling each other as they went.

They reached the bridge over the river just as the first, fat raindrops began to fall.

"Blast it all," Robert said.

"We must go back," Simon called from where he sat on the bridge with Nicholas, their legs dangling carelessly over the river.

The water was rushing furiously under the bridge, as high as Robert had ever seen it, and that feeling of uneasiness grew tenfold.

All of a sudden, it really didn't feel like a good idea to have Gina here.

"Yes," he agreed swiftly. "We must. Come, Gina."

Robert darted his glance around but couldn't see his sister.

The uneasiness grew instantly to foreboding.

"Gina!" he called, and James, Nicholas, and Simon began looking around, too.

"Gina, where are you?" he called.

"I'm here, you goose."

Robert whipped around, and an immediate fear clawed at him.

Gina was sitting atop a low branch of one of the many trees that bordered the river.

Robert had often stood on the same branch and jumped into the cool water of the river on hot summer days.

But it was far too dangerous for seven-year-old Gina to be on it, especially alone. And especially in the middle of a storm.

"Gina, come down here at once," he shouted, dashing over to the tree. "It isn't safe."

His impertinent little sister merely rolled her eyes.

"You always do it," she argued stubbornly.

"I am older," Robert said. "And the river is dangerous today."

"You sound just like Mama," Gina laughed.

"If you don't come down this instant, I will come up there and fetch you myself," Robert warned.

"Oh, Bobby –" How could a little girl sound so long-suffering? "You are so –"

It was a second, a split second. But long enough for Robert to know that something was terribly, terribly wrong.

There was a distinctive snap, and Gina's eyes widened with fear.

In the next moment, Robert watched the branch give, and though it took mere seconds, it felt like a lifetime.

There was only a short, terrified scream before the branch and his little sister crashed into the river below.

"Gina!"

One of the boys roared. It could have been him. It could have been James.

And Robert, God help him, hesitated.

Fear had him frozen in shock.

Only James brushing past brought him out of it.

His eyes couldn't look away. The branch bobbed to the surface and then seconds later, his sister's blonde curls appeared.

Finally, his brain kicked into action and he darted forward.

"What do we do?" Nicholas called in panic.

He heard James shout something, but he didn't pay any attention.

Without conscious thought, Robert ran to the bank and dove into the river.

Somewhere outside his bubble of terror, he knew the others were shouting his name.

The moment he hit the icy, tumultuous water, all the air left his body with the shock, and immediately the current gripped him.

It was so strong. Too strong.

Frantically, he looked around, even as the current tried to drag him under, to pull him away.

All he needed was just a glimpse of her.

There!

A flash of blonde against the greys and blacks surrounding him caught his eye.

Using all of his strength, Robert swam toward that flash of colour.

He prayed to God with all his might that he get there in time.

As though the Lord Himself had answered Robert's prayers, when he reached out, he managed to grab a handful of cotton from Gina's dress.

"I've got you," he shouted.

Gina was caught, her dress tangled in some reeds

on the riverbed.

Robert pulled her tiny body against his chest, terrified of the shivers wracking her body, oblivious to his own.

The rain lashed in earnest now, making it almost impossible to see, and the wind howled as though bemoaning the fate of the children by the riverside.

Gina was turning blue and gasping for breath.

"It's alright, Gina. I have you."

Robert repeated the litany over and over again even as he inwardly panicked.

How would he get her out of the water? How would he make sure she survived this waking nightmare?

"Robert!"

Robert looked up and saw James and Nicholas at the banks, mere feet above him.

Thank God.

Both boys lay down, their hands stretching toward Robert and Gina.

"Simon is gone for help," James shouted.

"We need to get her out of the water," Robert called back, not caring about anything else.

The others nodded their understanding.

Robert, with Herculean effort, tried to lift Gina toward James, but his little sister gripped desperately to his shoulders, her eyes wide with panic.

"Gina, you must let go," Robert shouted above the

wind, terror making his voice harsh.

"I-I c-can't!" She shivered, and Robert felt his eyes fill with tears.

This was beyond any horror he could ever imagine.

"You must," he insisted. "We need to get out of the water."

Gina stared at him for a moment, tears or rainwater streaming down her little face.

Finally, eons later, she nodded her head.

"Good girl," Robert said with relief as he felt her grip loosen.

But his fleeting relief was short-lived.

The second Gina's hands left his person, the unforgiving current snatched her body, and she shot away from him, as though pulled by an invisible whipcord.

"No!" Robert screamed, his hand darting out after her.

He managed to grip her fingertips, though both his and hers were icy with cold, and the merciless water rushed over their clasped hands, desperately trying to drag them apart.

"Pull me up," he yelled desperately.

He felt two pairs of hands on his jacket, as his cousin and his friend began the laborious task of pulling his drenched body from the water.

"Gina," he called, "hold on."

But he saw it then – the look that would haunt him for the rest of his miserable life. The look that no innocent child's eyes should hold. The look of someone who knew her life was about to end.

"Please," he sobbed. He couldn't even try to grab her tighter, could gain no more purchase on the bank or with her hand.

"Please, Gina. Hold on."

Though it should have been impossible with the cacophony of angry sounds the storm and river produced, Robert heard her whisper as clear as a bell. As clear as if she said it inside his very soul.

"Bobby, I'm scared."

Robert's heart clenched painfully. When Gina had been younger, she hadn't been able to pronounce the letter R properly and had taken to calling him Bobby. The name had stuck and became Gina's special name for him. She was the only one who used it and hearing it now from her blue, trembling lips was more painful than he could handle.

He couldn't speak. Could offer no word of comfort.

He began to pull against the hands dragging him to safety.

If Gina was going to let go, he would follow her. He wasn't going to watch her float away.

"Let go of me, James. She's slipping."

Perhaps they didn't hear. Perhaps they thought it better to save him, even though it was the worst thing they could do.

But they held on.

And Gina's grip loosened.

Within seconds, it was over.

Her tiny fingers slipped inevitably from his grasp.

Robert heard his own screams as though they came from someone else.

It was all so sudden.

One minute her tiny body floated, like a rag doll.

The next, it was gone, the river finally victorious in claiming a life.

Robert, on the bank now, fought with all his might to get away from the hands holding him back.

"Robert, she's gone. She's gone."

James' tearful voice sobbed in his ear as he clung furiously to his friend. But Robert wouldn't believe it. He couldn't.

Robert felt bile rise in his throat, and he turned toward the sodden ground, casting up his accounts.

Seconds or hours later, voices sounded all around him. Shouts of despair, screams of agony, yells of concern.

Someone threw a blanket around his shoulders and lifted him bodily into a cart.

Please, please, please don't let it be real. Please. Don't let it be real.

As the chills battered his body, Robert's head swam, and he prayed for the darkness that threatened on the edge of his consciousness. Welcomed it like an old friend.

He wanted it to come. And he wanted to remain in it forever.

Chapter One

ROBERT AWOKE WITH a start, jerking up in his bed, his skin glistening with sweat.

It took longer than usual for the blind panic to subside.

His heart pounded with remembered fear, and his mind replayed the expression on her face, the fear in her eyes, her fingers slipping through his over, and over, and over.

It had always been thus when the anniversary of Gina's death was approaching.

A death that he was responsible for.

That day had affected them all, he knew.

His father had taken to alcohol and become steadily more reliant on it as the years went on.

Robert had no doubt that was what had killed his sire eight years ago. That was the reason he was now the Duke of Montvale.

His mother was still alive, though existing might be a better description.

Her spirit had died the day Gina was swept away from them all, and she was nothing more than a shell of the person she'd once been.

Even his friends had been affected by Gina's death.

But then, Robert supposed, nobody could escape such a thing unscathed. Tragedies have a way of imprinting on one's soul. Something shifts inside you when you've lived through something awful. You go on with your life, but you're a different person than the one you once were.

And while James, Simon, and Nicholas had managed to recover from the drowning tolerably well, Robert couldn't go a day without the guilt and grief of that day gnawing at him.

Gina had been his sister, of course. But more than that – he'd been to blame.

Nobody had ever said so, but they didn't have to. He could see the indictment in the bottom of his father's empty brandy bottles, and in the sad vagueness of his mother's eyes, eyes that never quite focused on a person anymore.

Over the years, Robert had withdrawn more and more from his friends and loved ones.

He was fortunate, he supposed, in that Montvale Hall was situated in the stark, rugged isolation of Northumberland. Though the farmlands were hugely profitable and the village that owed its success to the estate was thriving, the Hall itself was set apart from everyone and everything, and Robert liked it that way.

He and his mother could stay here, haunted by the

things he didn't do to save Gina. Safe from pity and gossip.

Neither of them had ever been inclined to live at one of the other many houses he owned.

He kept only a skeletal staff. After all, there was only himself and his mother to take care of.

Montvale Hall had once hosted house parties, balls, and dinners to rival London in the height of the Season.

But no more.

It was now a haven for solitude and isolation. Dark, unforgiving. Like its master.

Robert wasn't deaf to the things that were said about him.

Servants talked. And townsfolk talked to servants.

He knew, for example, that people greatly pitied his mother for the hard life she had endured.

He knew also they had dubbed him the Monster of Montvale Hall.

A derisive grin, fleeting and unwelcome, crossed his face.

They weren't wrong, either. He was a monster of the worst kind. A monster responsible for the death of a child.

Robert scrubbed a hand over his face then jumped from the bed, filled with a restless agitation.

He knew that sleep would elude him for the remainder of the night. After a bad nightmare, sleep never again came. Or Robert never let it, in any case. Too terrified of what lurked behind his closed lids.

No, he would get no more rest this night.

Although, he acknowledged, as his storm-grey eyes took in the carriage clock on the mantle, it was already morning.

The household was still abed at this time, but in mere hours they would be up and bustling about, preparing a breakfast that would go largely untouched.

He moved to the window, pulling back the drapes to peer at the familiar landscape outside, gaining a sort of peace in the familiar view.

His rooms were at the back of the Hall. He'd relocated the master chamber as soon as he'd become the duke.

As far away from the view of the river as he could manage.

Now, all he saw were the acres and acres of his land. On a clear day, he'd be able to spy the rugged coastline in the distance.

How many times had he thought of running out there, toward the inevitable drop of the cliffs? Towards freedom from his torment?

Alas, he didn't have it in him. Whether that made him brave or cowardly, he had no idea. Perhaps just stupid.

Robert pressed the heel of his hand against his forehead. Usually after a nightmare, his head began to pound.

He'd be tempted to drown himself in whiskey, but he actually needed his wits about him today.

For today, James would arrive, seeking a favour.

His note had been mysterious. James had written to say he was coming to stay, and he was bringing along something that needed looking after. Shamelessly begging favours.

Robert had felt a twinge of curiosity.

As the influential Marquess of Avondale, James's power was only a step below Robert's own. And he was rich as Croesus, having inherited all of his family's old money and then expanding on it with business interests here and in the Americas.

What on earth could he need from Robert?

The gentlemen had remained close over the intervening years. Along with Simon and Nicholas. Or as close as Robert would allow, in any case.

Contrary to Robert's desperate attempts to distance himself from his three friends, the tragedy that had befallen Gina had sealed their fates. Simply put, living through such an ordeal had created a bond that even Robert's best attempts could not break.

After Gina's death, Robert had barely spoken to any of them. Yet when he'd returned to Eton, every day they were at his door, dragging him into life again. At Oxford, they had done the same. And when they'd each ascended to their titles – two dukes, a marquess, and an earl – they'd reached an unspoken agreement not to speak of the tragedy.

It was the only reason Robert remained friends with them. And though he rarely, if ever, admitted it, their friendship had been the only thing that had kept him alive all those years ago. And he was grateful for it. Then and now.

Though the young men didn't see each other often, he knew that James had continued to be quite sickeningly *good* throughout his life. A paragon the matrons of the *ton* flung their daughters at with abandon and debutantes simpered and swooned about.

Nicholas, too, had grown to become a favourite of Society. Though the main seat of his duchy was in Ireland, he spent almost all of his time in London, even during the summer months when most people disappeared to enjoy the sunshine in their country homes or in Bath or Brighton by the sea.

Simon was, by all accounts, as debauched and rakish as he had always claimed he would be. And Robert was secretly pleased that of the four of them, he wasn't the only one with a blackened soul.

The first rays of brilliant orange began to rise over the clifftops, signalling the start of another interminable day.

Robert negated to summon his valet, preferring to dress himself.

He would ring for a pot of strong coffee and then

go for an early morning ride, careful to avoid the river as he always was.

Then he could return and wonder what on earth James could want from him.

James, he knew, was only just returning from the Americas after a prolonged stay.

He had written that he was going to break his journey with Simon in Liverpool before travelling on to visit Robert.

A swift smile once again lit Robert's face. James and Simon were a study in opposites.

If Robert was a monster then Simon, Earl of Dashford, was certainly the Devil he'd been labelled as.

Without doubt, James and Nicholas were veritable saints compared to the sinners that were Robert and Simon.

Still, Robert was the one James wanted the favour from.

Perhaps it was a sort of familial connection, though they weren't blood relatives. Perhaps it was yet another ruse of James's to surreptitiously check on him, an attempt to convince him yet again to join the land of the living.

The Season was approaching, Robert knew. Another that he ignored, wilfully abandoning his duties at Parliament.

Robert donned his charcoal grey superfine, tying his cravat haphazardly. No doubt his valet would hunt him down and fix it at some point, but for now, Robert just wanted to escape the confines of the house, which was larger than most but somehow felt oppressively small.

Making his way toward the stables, Robert acknowledged the various greetings from stable hands and grooms with a silent nod.

Nobody would ever accuse him of being friendly and chatty, but neither would he ignore hardworking members of his household.

Arriving at the stables and calling for his mount, Storm, Robert inhaled the tangy air that always held the salty reminder that he lived close to the sea.

Strangely, the unforgiving sea didn't scare him. In fact, he loved the rugged, dangerous coastline that bordered his estate. It often mirrored his mood and was a comforting reminder that he was just one, insignificant person surrounded by a huge, if unforgiving world.

The unmistakeable whinny of his black stallion snapped Robert out of his musings, and he mounted the steed before turning toward the wide expanse of fields where he could give the horse his head.

It would be some hours before James arrived, begging his favour. And with Robert's mood blacker than usual, he was inclined to refuse before he even knew what the favour was.

Chapter Two

"WELL IT IS certainly different from New York."

Abigail Langton smiled ruefully at her companion, who sat across from her in the plush carriage.

James Harring, Marquess of Avondale, smiled back at her.

"That is because we are in the wilds of Northumberland, Abby. London will be more like what you're used to, I expect."

"Yet you insist that we come here first," she countered, raising a brow slightly.

In truth, as the bustle of Liverpool, where they'd stayed a couple of days with James's friend Lord Dashford, gave way to the more rugged landscapes of the North of England, Abby felt her excitement mounting.

Now that they'd entered the county of Northumberland, she'd almost cricked her neck trying to take in the craggy beauty around her.

She'd never seen such a beautiful place in her life. It seemed to speak to her very soul.

In fact, she'd been feeling that way since they'd first docked in the country of her mother's birth.

"I did," James said stoutly, unrepentantly. "I told you, it's bad enough that we even stayed with Simon without another female in attendance. And it's positively ruinous that you travelled alone with me from America in the first place. If the *ton* finds out, your life here in England will be over before it's begun."

"And hiding me away in – what did you call it?" She frowned in confusion, and James grinned again.

"Northumberland."

"Right." Abby nodded. "Northumberland." A bit of a mouthful, but she'd get used to it. "As I was saying, hiding me away here first will mean I'm respectable?"

"I'm not hiding you away. But you cannot show up at Town for a Season without a reputable sponsor."

"And that's not you?"

James laughed.

"No, that is most certainly not me."

"But aren't you rather a big deal here? Mother said you were."

"Yes, I am. But I am also male. And single."

"And my cousin," Abby reminded him. "Practically a brother."

"How you feel about me, and I you, has very little to do with it."

Abby sighed and shook her head, dislodging a

golden blonde strand from her chignon.

The maid James had insisted on hiring for propriety's sake, who was currently sitting atop their conveyance since she didn't travel well, would be angry with her.

Abigail had yet to go an entire day without doing damage to her maid's attempts at styling her hair.

"I will never understand your stuffy customs, James."

"They're not my customs. They are the customs of the *beau monde*. And if you want to experience a London Season, which you claimed to do *loudly,* then you have to follow the rules."

"Very well," she sighed. In the next moment, however, she brightened considerably. "I don't care how I get there, as long as I get there."

James grinned indulgently.

"I'm only sorry I don't have any sisters, my dear. If I did, we could have gone directly to London and gotten you ready."

"I suppose if you're not an appropriate chaperone, then Thomas is definitely out of the question," Abby grinned.

She'd never met her cousin Thomas, James's younger brother.

And she'd only met James because he had business in New York that he'd oversee.

It had been destiny, she'd told him the day she'd

begged him to escort her back to London. The fates wanted her in England.

"The fates might," James had quipped. "But I'm sure your parents don't."

Abby hadn't quite known how to explain that she had been little more than a thorn in her mother's side ever since her birth.

Mrs. Langton was an inherent snob whose life's ambition was to ensure that everyone around her knew she was the epitome of high society. Blue-blooded English stock, the daughter of a marquess.

As a wilful youth, she'd found it terribly romantic to run away to America with a wealthy merchant's son.

However, it hadn't taken long for her to realise she desperately missed the rolling green hills of England and, more importantly, the sycophantic fawning that came with being the daughter of a powerful Peer.

Unfortunately for the newly-married Mrs. Langton, she had become pregnant with Abigail only months later, and her fate had been sealed.

Which was how Abby had become a source of regret and bitterness for both her parents, though her father made the effort to hide it occasionally. In her father's defence, he hadn't always been uncaring of Abigail. In truth, he'd rather doted on her in her earliest memories. But, Abby supposed that years of his wife's obvious unhappiness, and Abigail being one of the main sources of it, had worn the man down. And so it was that he had come to care as little as his wife did.

Abigail knew their disastrous history because it was one of her mother's favourite stories to tell.

"And the duchess doesn't mind sponsoring me?" Abby asked now, refusing to give her uncaring mother any more headspace.

James had told her very little, save that the dowager duchess had only a son and would benefit greatly from a young lady to go about London with.

Plus, being the particular friend of the Duchess of Montvale would open every conceivable door to her, James had said.

When she'd first put the proposal to her cousin, whom she'd only met a year ago but who had already come to be like a brother to her, he'd steadfastly refused.

There was no way he was taking her across the Atlantic with him to jolly old England. No, he didn't care that she was positively desperate for a famed English Season. No, he didn't care that she dreamed of seeing the land she read so much about in her ridiculous romantic novels. No, he didn't care that it was high time she found a husband, and that as the granddaughter and now cousin of the esteemed Marquess of Avondale, she really should marry a Peer.

And poor James had naïvely thought that was the end of the matter.

But Abby had long since had a reputation of being able to get her own way, whether through winsome smiles, pretty pouts, or good old-fashioned manipulation.

She'd engaged in all three zealously until she'd worn James down and he'd helped her convince her mother, his aunt, that it would be a good idea.

Their journey across the Atlantic had been dull as ditch water. James had barely allowed her to leave the cabin he'd procured for her. And never, ever without her maid.

It had been a long and arduous journey and not one that she relished completing.

Well, perhaps she'd fall in love with an English lord and would end up making her home here rather than make the return journey, though she couldn't imagine never seeing her sisters again.

Her poor sisters hadn't fared much better than Abby when it came to their mother's regard. She had done her duty, providing more children to her husband, though she had never managed to give him the son he so craved.

It had been left to Abigail to provide any and all real love and affection to her sisters. But they were no longer very young. In fact, Alison had already come of age, and Elizabeth wouldn't be far behind. So, much as Abby knew how terribly she would miss them, she had to think of her own future. Maybe her sisters could even visit, when she got herself settled somewhere.

Abby smiled to herself. Her mother would no doubt shake her head at her eldest daughter's romantic nonsense. And resent her even more for having the life she, herself, had thrown away.

"Not at all," James said jovially enough, though Abby thought she sensed a tightening around his mouth.

"You're sure?" she pressed.

Did he hesitate a moment? It seemed he hesitated a moment.

"Of course. Ah, we are almost here."

That sounded suspiciously like changing the subject, but Abby was suitably distracted.

She turned toward the window and gasped at the beauty of the coastline. The lush green of the verdant grass interspersed with outcroppings of rock, and stone disappeared into a vista of the startling blue of the ocean that seemed to go on forever.

"Montvale Hall is one of the most beautifully situated houses in the country," James explained. "Though "house" doesn't really do it justice."

"Is it as big as Avondale Abby?" Abigail asked.

Her younger sisters had been vastly amused to know that the seat of their cousin had the same name as their sister.

"Bigger," James said with a wry smile.

"It is very kind of the duke to allow us to impose on him for almost four weeks," Abigail said, eyes still on the landscape.

If she had looked at James then, she would have seen him pull guiltily at his cravat.

"Well, he is family," James said, and there was that strange expression on his face again.

A prickle of unease ran along Abby's spine.

"Your family," she corrected. "Not mine. And not really, come to that. You aren't actually related."

"Nevertheless, it will be good for the dowager to have you there. He will see that."

Abigail frowned at the cryptic remark but before she could question anything else, they passed through two massive wrought iron gates and onto the long driveway toward the Hall.

She resisted the urge to stick her head out the window in order to catch a glimpse of the house.

Finally, after an age, the carriage pulled up to a circular driveway, centred by an ominous looking fountain.

Abigail felt her jaw drop at the image in front of her.

The place was a fortress, and it really did nothing for Abby's sudden unease.

Learn more about
The Saints & Sinners series
by going here.
nadinemillard.com/saints-and-sinners

About Nadine Millard

Nadine Millard is a bestselling writer hailing from Dublin, Ireland.

When she's not writing historical romance, she's managing her chaotic household of three children, a husband and a very spoiled dog!

She's a big fan of coffee and wine with a good book and will often be found at her laptop at 2am when a book idea strikes.

Connect with Nadine!
Website: nadinemillard.com
Newsletter: eepurl.com/dNCiX-
BookBub: bookbub.com/authors/nadine-millard
Amazon: amazon.com/Nadine-Millard/e/B00JA9OXFK
Facebook: facebook.com/nadinemillardauthor

Made in the USA
Las Vegas, NV
21 December 2021